Praise for Candy Caine

BECAUSE OF YOU "...Engrossing...a page turner... I would recommend this book!" — Romance Novels in Color "A sweet romance. I love the heartwarming ending." — Library Thing

FLAVOR OF THE WEEK "Pure light-hearted fun. A really heart-warming read with endearing characters." — LBAS Book Blog

FOR YOUR LOVE "...A cast of well-crafted characters you'll want to cheer for...delightful story..." — Niambi Brown Davis, Author of Sanctuary "A sexy, fabulous read. I couldn't put it down." — Bertrice Small, New York Times bestselling author

MORE HEATED PLEASURES "...Candy Caine once again hits the right erotic sweet spots..." — Cynthia White, author of Awakened Desire "A roller coaster ride of erotic thrills... Great fun!" — Alice Gaylord, author of The Reluctant Handyman

NO STRINGS ATTACHED "Good quick read with sex, secrets, and trauma." — Reading By The Book

SAVE THE LAST DANCE FOR ME "A story about real relationships...the romance between Evie and Dillon is electric. Candy Caine's writing is impressive." — Latrivia S. Nelson, bestselling author of The Ugly Girlfriend

Also by Candy Caine

The Life and Loves of Ariel Jones, I, Erogenous Jones Volume 1
Ariel and Ray Uncensored The Life and Loves of Ariel Jones, Volume 2
At First Sight
Because of You
Christmas with a Stranger
Dangerous Attraction
Flavor of the Week
For Your Love
Forever Yours
Heated Pleasures
It's Love That Really Counts
Justify My Love
Love with a Younger Man
More Heated Pleasures
Never Is Not Forever
No Strings Attached
Save the Last Dance for Me
Softly, As I Leave You
Forever in My Heart
Coming Soon: Accidental Love

FOR THE LOVE OF MONEY

By

Candy Caine

PROLOGUE

Leonardo da Vinci Airport, Rome 1985

Lena Bianchi sat in the Leonardo da Vinci Airport watching the clock next to the Arrivals board. There was an open paperback on her lap, but she'd already given up on trying to read. She was too excited to concentrate. Paolo, her husband of two years, was due to arrive in ten minutes.

With her bulk, it would take longer for her to get to the baggage area where she was to meet him, so she hauled herself up from the chair and began to make her way through the crowd of people, coming and going. Pregnant with twins, her ninth month couldn't go fast enough. It was like carrying around a fifty-pound stone.

The announcement of the arrival of Paolo's flight came just as she entered the baggage area. Exhausted from her long walk, she sat down on the first empty bench she found facing the entrance to wait for him.

Paolo entered ten minutes later and Lena rose to greet him. He saw her and the sight of his huge smile warmed her as she hurried into his open arms. Just as they embraced, there was a tremendous bang and the entire building shook. They looked up to see the roof of the baggage claim area collapse on top of them. A steel shard pierced Paolo's back, his body falling onto Lena's, shielding her from most of the debris.

Later, as the relief workers sifted through the rubble for survivors, Lena had regained consciousness and heard them. All she cared about was saving her babies. When a worker came near enough to hear her, she called out and wiggled the fingers of her only free hand. It was just enough for the man to see and hear her.

"Hey! Over here! I found someone alive!" he shouted as he began to pull Paolo's body off of her.

Airlifted to the nearest hospital, the life was ebbing from Lena. One of the EMTs noticed and called out, "Her pressure's dropping!"

"We've got to deliver her babies now," the other said, wiping the perspiration from Lena's dusty skin.

By the time the helicopter touched down at the hospital, the healthy cries of two newborn baby girls with café au lait colored skin could be heard. Lena lived just long enough to know her children were alive and safe.

CHAPTER ONE

Present Day, Fountain Hills, Arizona

Vanessa Jeffers was putting on her makeup, deciding whether or not to put foundation on her flawless café au lait skin. She was co-hosting one of her charities for needy children. She'd hoped that her husband, Jake, would be able to accompany her, but he begged off with the excuse of meeting with a new client. With the divorce rate on the rise and his being one of the most sought out divorce lawyers in Arizona, she wasn't surprised, merely disappointed.

Vanessa did a great deal to help children. They were her passion. Whether they were impoverished or orphans, they became her surrogate kids. Married to Jake for five years, she'd had a miscarriage and had never been able to conceive again. Jake hadn't wanted to adopt, so Vanessa quietly accepted her childless fate. Throwing her energies into helping children seemed to help her cope with not having children of her own. Jake disliked children. He found them a burden and a useless drain on funds. With a child, you couldn't just pick up at a given notice and go on vacation. Not wanting to mold his life around a child's needs, Jake simply didn't want to be a parent.

Vanessa tried to understand his point of view, but found it quite difficult, for to her, children were a blessing. Now knowing how Jake felt about children, perhaps it was a good thing she hadn't conceived.

As for the gala that evening, Vanessa had made a last-minute effort to have Jake escort her to the dinner, but he declined, again saying he had to meet with the new client. He could have gone with her, for she had told him about this evening at least two months ago. It was obvious that he really didn't want to go. In fact, he'd been attending her galas less and less lately. Which made her wonder...

Was it because of her? Had he found her less desirable? Why would he? She hadn't changed. Still willowy with shapely legs, her smooth, flawless café au lait complexion radiated youth. People told her all the time how young she looked. She applied mascara to her velvety-long lashes that surrounded her hazel-green, almond-shaped eyes. Now she began to add a hint of blush to her delicate, high cheekbones that gave her a somewhat exotic look. She smiled to herself as she recalled Jake comparing her to a sleek, black panther. Of course, he hadn't realized the double meaning, but she had. She pushed a wayward lock of her shoulder length, dark-brown hair from her face.

Had Jake grown bored with her? With all the philandering going on in the circles she traveled, there was always some fresh scandal being discussed at the luncheons. Of course, she never expected Jake to cheat on her. His behavior didn't suggest it, either. He rarely came home late and was at home waiting for her when she had. Perhaps she's reading too much into Jake's unwillingness to attend her charitable functions. And then there was the fact he was not as sexually active lately. She smiled at the thought of how he'd take her anywhere in the house during the early years of their marriage. Was there another woman? She really didn't want to go there and dismissed the thought.

Jake walked Vanessa to the front door and kissed her cheek. "Have a good time and raise a lot of money."

***

Vanessa had been pleased with the amount of money raised for the Phoenix Children's Hospital. The dinner and Chinese auction had gone well without a hitch. Now, as she slipped her key into the lock of their beautiful home perched in the mountains of Fountain Hills, she looked forward to sharing this news with Jake. She took off her jacket and hung it in the hall closest before stopping to peek in their den. He wasn't there or in his office.

She found him in their king-sized bed, propped up against the headboard, reading through a brief. Vanessa actually felt sorry for the spouse that Jake would no doubt destroy both emotionally and financially. He was a formidable litigator who worked with a team of crack investigators. He hated to lose and won more often than not in and out of court.

Vanessa's heart filled as she saw him there looking so handsome and virile. His bare chest showcasing his six-pack, gave her a jolt of excitement. At thirty-six, his black hair sported streaks of gray at his temples, but his deep blue eyes still sparkled like rare gems. Small crease lines appeared at their corners whenever he smiled. And when he smiled, it reminded Vanessa of the past when things between them were better. Her gaze fell on his sensuous mouth, whose kisses she needed more of.

Jake sensed his wife's entrance and looked up. "You're home, early. Have a good time?"

"Yes. We raised enough money to buy several new imaging machines."

"I'm glad your night was successful."

"I was hoping that I could catch you before you went to sleep," Vanessa said. Jake looked at her expectantly.

"We...we haven't spent much time together, lately."

"And whose fault is that? I've been here while you've been gallivanting around town trying to save the world's children."

"That's not fair!" Vanessa said as tears began to well in her eyes. It forced her to turn away a moment while she tried to keep them from falling.

"Really? You still haven't learned that it will never fill the place of a child," Jake said harshly. "It's time to move on. Besides, charity begins at home."

Tears began to stream down Vanessa's face. "That's not why I do it."

Jake opened his arms. His voice and demeanor softened. "I know. Come here, baby. I'm sorry. I shouldn't have said that. It's just that I'm so damn tired of being here alone all the time."

And I'm the one who wants a child so much, Vanessa thought as she buried her face in Jake's broad chest. *And you're the one who couldn't give a damn.*

"Shh." He stroked her back and kissed the top of her head. "I should not have been so harsh. I'm sorry."

As Jake stroked her, Vanessa soon felt a different sensation. Her heart raced and there was that familiar tug she always felt in her sex. He gently lifted her chin so he could plant kisses on her forehead, eyes and finally, her lips. The first kiss was soft and light. But the next was a longer, more sensual one in which his tongue sent shivers of desire racing through her. When their lips parted, her mouth burned with fire as Jake bent to kiss the pulsing at the base of her throat.

By the time Jake reached around to unzip her dress, Vanessa had forgotten her sadness. It had been replaced by wanting and a need only Jake could fulfill. She got off the bed and let her black Valentino dress fall to the floor. When she began to slip off her three inch Manolo Blahniks, Jake whispered hoarsely, "Don't. Leave them on."

Jake pushed everything off the bed as Vanessa got back on wearing only her shoes. As he reached for her, the tenting in his pajama bottom whetted her appetite. Knowing it was synonymous with his desire for her, she felt like the luckiest woman in the world.

Vanessa pushed Jake back down onto his back as their lips met in a hungry kiss that sent new spirals of pleasure through her and a swirling sensation in the pit of her stomach. As his lips slid down her neck to her breasts, the tug in her sex grew stronger. Vanessa moaned softly. Jake continued to lick and suck her nipples for several more minutes. He knew this was driving her wild.

Jake rolled her onto her back and loomed over her, a smile on his lips as he saw the wanting in his wife's eyes. She reached to stroke his penis, but he pulled out of her reach to torment her. He knew a little torment would stimulate her even more. Sure enough, as he nipped one nipple and kneaded the other, her body appeared to buck involuntarily.

As he planted tiny kisses down Vanessa's body, Jake grew harder watching her body lift off the bed in pleasure. He loved the sexual power he had over her...and the others. Knowing her inner thighs were most sensitive, he homed in on one, kissing and lightly licking the tender skin causing Vanessa to squirm. Then he did the same to the other. Vanessa could hardly contain herself.

Jake took his time, knowing Vanessa was probably near the boiling point with desire. He lifted Vanessa's long, shapely legs onto his shoulders and gently kissed and nibbled her inner thighs. Then he began to run the flat end of his tongue all around her sex, but avoiding touching it. Vanessa's body bucked as she tried to move his head closer. Her patience was wearing thin and yet Jake continued to torment her with pleasure—just not the way she wanted it.

He continued to run his tongue from her ass to the opening of her vagina. Then he ran along the outside of her engorged labia, avoiding contact with her clitoris. Vanessa's body trembled. "Please, Jake, suck me," she finally cried out. Knowing she was so close, he obliged her.

Jake began to suck Vanessa's clitoris. She was now moaning loudly and thrashing her head from side to side as she mashed her sex into Jake's face. As he gently tugged her clitoris, her entire body began to spasm. He continued to pleasure her until she was spent. After spending several hours with his mistress, Cheryl, who had the sexual appetite of two women and drained every last drop of his semen, he really hadn't wanted to fuck Vanessa, too. He'd been with Cheryl that afternoon and hadn't lied to Vanessa about waiting for her all night.

Sure, he loved Vanessa. Only he loved her inheritance more. He made big bucks, but it could never be enough. Besides, he'd wanted to retire early and enjoy life. Therefore, Jake would just about do anything to ensure that his wife's inheritance would remain half his.

So he continued his husbandly duties and kept Vanessa happy. Satiated, she curled up against him and fell asleep. Jake eased himself out of bed, trying not to wake her. He padded into the bathroom to brush his teeth and prepare for bed. By the time he returned, Vanessa was sound asleep. Jake smiled at the sight. She looked so peaceful. He thought himself quite the stud and gave himself a mental pat on the back.

Slipping under the covers on his side of the bed, Jake got into bed. His mind drifted to that afternoon with Cheryl and the promises he'd made to her—promises he'd probably never keep.

CHAPTER TWO

The following day, Jake met with a new client, a forty-year-old woman who had been recommended to him by a friend who happened to be a most satisfied customer, coming away from the divorce Jake brokered with three-quarters of the goodies she'd desired. And the alimony her former husband was now paying was a substantial amount. Of course, this new client expected the same, if not more. Obviously, Jake couldn't produce the same results all the time, but he came damn near close. This was the stuff of which made him the go-to divorce lawyer in the eastern half of Arizona.

The woman was late. This annoyed Jake, who actually considered his time to be money. As he sat at his desk in his Gatsbyesque Art Deco adorned office surrounded by furniture that could have come straight from the twenties, with its strong geometric shapes and colors, he stared mindlessly at a painting by Tamara de Lempicke, a Polish Baroness who settled in Paris after the Russian Revolution. Her paintings of many prominent people, with its bold, bright colors and angular style, was an excellent example of Art Deco. Jake mused how he could have played the part of Jay Gatsby, F.Scott Fitzgerald's most memorable character, to perfection. He admired the *chutzpah* and reveled in the glamour and luxury of the period. Too bad it was his lousy luck to be born during the following century with its lackluster style.

His receptionist, Trudy, buzzed him on the office intercom. "Mrs. Simmons has arrived," she said in her soft midwestern voice. Hearing her voice, even through the intercom, always brought a smile to his lips. As nice as it was to listen to Trudy Rudd, it was even more of a pleasure to look at her silky blonde hair, creamy-white skin and cornflower blue eyes. With her willowy body, Trudy could wear anything and still be a sight to behold. Though he'd love to see her in a sheer teddy with garters and heels, she was one woman who was off limits to him—unless she decided to divorce the body builder she was married to.

The blonde-haired woman who walked into his office could be the poster child for the American Plastic Surgery Association. From her obvious boob job to her pillowed lips, Jake wondered if there were any original parts left on her body.

He rose to greet her at the door. "Mrs. Simmons. I'm Jake Jeffers," he said, gesturing to the chair in front of his desk. Please have a seat. Can I get you something to drink?"

"No. I'm fine, thank you," she said in an affected voice. Her eyes took him all in, slowly working their way up from his polished Italian leather shoes to his tailored, navy blue pinstripe suit and solid red silk tie. When her eyes reached his, Jake tried to read them. He thought he deciphered a strange mix of lust, need, and knowing. Was she giving him the eye and flirting with him? Other women had done the same, but discovered early he didn't mix business with pleasure. A client was a client and nothing more. Hopefully, Mrs. Simmons would learn that quickly. Mentally sighing, if not, he'd just have to settle her case in record time.

Over the years, Jake had developed an introductory set of questions that helped him proceed with each divorce filing. Since there was no one-fit-all strategy, because every case was different, these questions were quite comprehensive. Depending on the answers he received, he devised a strategy which he used to proceed.

"May I call you Olivia?" he began.

In a more deep, sultry voice, she replied, "Why of course."

Jake smiled. "Olivia, in order to best proceed, I have a set of comprehensive questions that I'd like to ask you. Please answer as best you can and as honestly as you can. Okay?"

She nodded. "Ask away. I'm in your *capable* hands. And, if it gets me all I want, all the better."

Jake wasn't certain what to make of her attitude. She'd made it sound as if she was doing him a favor. He had to remind himself it wasn't his job to judge her, but facilitate her divorce. Therefore, he jumped right into the questionnaire, which took a good part of an hour. At the conclusion, Olivia stood and slowly straightened her skirt. "Will you be needing further assistance from me?

"If you mean to update you on my progress—"

"Not exactly. I just want you to know that I'm *available* whenever you need me."

"We're only just starting at this point. You've given me a wealth of information and I have to see how I can use it to the best of my abilities. After that, if I do need any more information I will get in touch with you."

"That's all I wanted to know, but if you need me, remember, I'm available."

He watched her leave. Her words and mannerisms made him feel quite uncomfortable. He knew a woman on the make when he saw one. She definitely had an agenda. Therefore, the sooner he settled her divorce suit, the better.

Jake instructed Trudy that he was leaving the office for the rest of the afternoon. He'd called Cheryl and told her to meet him at their usual place for a drink. First libations and then sex would help him recover from the time spent with Olivia Simmons. Just thinking about it made him feel better.

***

Olivia Simmons was already fixated on Jake Jeffers. In her mind, he would make the perfect next husband. One would think that the gold band on his finger would nix such an idea, but it did not faze Olivia. Being in the prime of her life, she considered herself an excellent catch. She was intelligent and had oodles of money to sweeten things. And yes, she was most benevolent. Instead of removing her first two husbands by murderous means, she chose divorce. Her first lawyer had a fatal heart attack and left her high and dry. Luckily, she discovered Jake Jeffers to replace him. Yes, she decided he'd make a wonderful replacement in so many ways.

A realist at heart, Olivia knew it would take time to win the love of a married man. She would be patient and follow her well-choreographed plan of action. Everything she did was pre-calculated, because she feared being wrong and making mistakes. In fact, she'd spent hours trying on suits and dresses until she found the one that looked the best on her before leaving the house.

Determined to win Jake Jeffers's affection and add him to her growing string of husbands, she wouldn't give up easily. That wasn't her style.

***

Cheryl Ames was a high-class escort. If she'd lived during the sixteenth century, she would have made an excellent courtesan. Classy and knowledgeable with beauty and audacity to match, she'd been well sought out by gentlemen before her path crossed with Jake Jeffers. He found this red-haired beauty to be one of the most exciting women he'd ever been with. Each time they'd meet, it always felt as thrilling as the first time and often even better.

Jake quickly concluded that he didn't care to share this woman with other men so he made her a proposition. He would set her up in a condo in a luxurious complex in Phoenix if she made herself available to him whenever he wanted her. As good as it sounded, Cheryl didn't readily agree to this arrangement. Instead, she held out for a substantial allowance, as well. It wasn't beneath her to use her beauty to get exactly what she wanted. Oh, she wanted Jake, too, but she was costly and he'd have to pay her price or not have her at all.

Cheryl had been born dirt poor on a farm in Idaho. She learned, though, at a young age to use her feminine wiles to her advantage. Even though she'd done her research and knew Jake was a womanizer and married, she still hitched her wagon to him with the hope to eventually cash in on his wealth. She was well aware of his reputation as an aggressive, successful lawyer and his wife's money which made him even more enticing. She'd crossed paths with Vanessa Jeffers at more than one charitable gala when she was an escort.

Before she met Jake, Cheryl was able to separate her business from her feelings. Despite not wanting to, she fell in love with the man. However, she was quite the consummate actress and was able to restrain herself. If she hadn't, she might forfeit the upper hand in their relationship. And that she would never do.

Now sitting in front of her mirror as she prepared to meet Jake, Cheryl stared at her reflection. She feared finding a line or other blemish to mar her beauty. Without her looks, she'd have nothing. Her rich, glowing auburn hair was natural and hung in long graceful curves over her porcelain shoulders. It intensified her large green eyes. Her lips were full and she was blessed with straight white teeth. Having a fair complexion, she had highlighted her fine cheekbones with blush. Along her narrow nose was a light smattering of tiny freckles which she covered with foundation. The dimple in her chin finished her oval-shaped face. She picked up an expensive bottle of perfume from her dressing table and dabbed a little behind her ears before slipping expensive two-carat diamond studs in them.

Satisfied with how she looked, she stood and straightened the hem of her clingy, black silk dress. One last look in the mirror and she was good to go. She picked up her purse and light wrap and headed out to the garage where she kept her bright apple-red, two-seater Mercedes. She was going to meet Jake at their usual place, Club 73.

Club 73 was a small bistro type restaurant/bar off of Saguaro Boulevard. It was tucked away in the middle of a strip mall on a busy commercial Street in Fountain Hills. The stucco building had been there as long as Jake could remember and the bistro's claim to fame was their perfect Margaritas. Though he was a bourbon man at heart, he placated Cheryl who loved Margaritas. However, that wasn't the true reason they often met there. No one he knew ever frequented the place. Nor did any of his acquaintances ever stay in the small no-tell motel nearby where he and Cheryl often ended up.

To Vanessa, Jake was the dutiful husband and he aimed to keep it that way. As long as she remained clueless about his extramarital affairs, the better. If she divorced him, her money would be lost. He knew he was playing with fire, but he liked living on the edge. It kept his blood roaring through his veins and his taste for different women, fulfilled.

Jake arrived first and took a seat at their usual table in the corner of the dimly lit bar. It was a small place and most of the stools at the long bar were taken, as well as many of the round tables being waited on by a scantily clad waitress.

He was nursing his first drink when Cheryl walked through the front door. Watching her hips sway as she slowly approached him gave him a rush. She always had that affect on him. Cheryl was the most exciting sexual creature he'd ever met. He took the length of her in, eying how the black dress clung to her curves. He could feel his heart banging around in his chest and found it hard to breathe as a certain part of his anatomy twitched. Hopefully, she'd only want a drink and not a meal before they left. He could hardly wait to get her into his arms.

Rising to greet her, she gave him a passionate kiss. For Jake, that was a good sign that she wanted him, too.

"You look lovely," Jake said, signaling the waitress.

Cheryl rewarded him with one of her Hollywood smiles.

"What can I get you?" the waitress said.

Holding up his glass, he said, "Another for me and a Margarita for her."

"Are you hungry or would you like room service later on?" Jake asked Cheryl.

She cocked her head and gave him an enigmatic smile. "Now what do you think I want?"

"Hopefully, me," Jake said as the waitress placed their drinks on the table.

"I *always* want you. Tell me, how was your day?"

"The usual. From my perspective, the institute of marriage is breaking down— not that I'm complaining mind you. But when it does, the people involved can be so vindictive. I wonder why anybody gets married today."

"Obviously, so they can get a divorce and make you rich."

Jake raised an eyebrow and shook his head. "Sometimes you say the sweetest things."

Cheryl laughed her deep throaty laugh. Jake couldn't help himself and joined her. They continued the light banter as Cheryl ran her foot seductively up Jake's leg.

"Would you like another drink or would you like to get going?"

She gave him that enigmatic smile again.

He rose and left a $50 bill on the table. In his best Humphrey Bogart voice, he said, "Let's go, sweetheart."

They linked arms and headed out to the parking lot where they'd split up and each drive their car over to the Desert Motel nearby. It was the type of "no tell" motel that charged by the hour. Even so, the sheets were clean and no one, either of them knew frequented the place.

Jake got there first. Cheryl pulled into the lot several minutes later and waited for Jake to come out with the key. He left his car in the lot and got into Cheryl's Mercedes.

"We're in 109. It should be the last room around to the right."

"I see it," Cheryl said and eased the car into a spot close to the room.

Together, they walked to the door and Jake opened it. Cheryl entered and waited until he closed the door behind him before throwing her arms around his neck and kissing him passionately.

"Hey! It's only been two days since I last saw you. Do you miss me that much?"

She took his hand and led him toward the bed. "A day without you is a day without sunshine—and sex."

Jake chuckled. "Why don't you show me just how much you missed me."

Cheryl dropped to her knees and slowly unzipped the fly on his slacks. "A picture is worth a thousand words," she said, reaching inside for his penis.

Jake's erection grew in her hand as she stroked it. He made a soft guttural sound which brought a smile to her lips. She went down on him, taking the length of him into her mouth. As she pleasured him, she stroked his balls several minutes before she sucked and licked them. Jake moaned. Cheryl knew he was at his most vulnerable state and savored the power she now had over him. Taking the length of him back into her mouth, she'd continue to suck him until he orgasmed. Once he came, he'd be so willing to please her.

"That's it baby," he half-moaned. "Yes, don't stop."

Jake began to twitch indicating he was about to ejaculate. Once Cheryl had overcome her antipathy for swallowing, she became quite adept. It was over in moments and now it was her turn.

"Mmm, you're the best," Jake said, nuzzling her neck.

"I know."

"Such modesty," Jake said, drawing her close to him.

They stood in front of the bed kissing as they slowly undressed one another. Cheryl was practically creaming in her panties, wanting to feel Jake inside her. Luckily for her, the man had stamina— more than most men. By the time they were naked and on top of the bed, his erection was hard and ready to please her.

Cheryl needed little foreplay. She was primed and ready for him. She was well aware that that was one thing that Jake loved about her. No matter what, when or where, she was always turned on. Unfortunately, there was the other side of the coin, so to speak, being that because she was so sexually charged, there were times that she wasn't truly satisfied. However, to admit this to Jake would be to say he was less of the stud he considered himself. She knew better than to go there. Men had such fragile egos.

As Jake slid his cock into her slick, wet pussy, she purred in contentment. Cheryl grabbed his ass and pushed him deeper into her. Lifting her own ass, she shoved a pillow under it to add a little height. He got the message and pump harder and faster. Making love with Cheryl was like going to the gym. He was glad he was in shape. How stupid would it be to take such precautions to prevent Vanessa from finding out about his dalliances and then die in the arms of a woman because he was overweight? Of course Jake knew better. As far as he was concerned, his body was a temple and women worshiped at it.

Jake's thoughts were interrupted by Cheryl's vocalization which was now loud moaning indicating that she was going to come. He plunged into her snatch as deep as he could and was rewarded with an elongated moan from her pillow lips as her body spasmed. He didn't dare stop until she was still.

CHAPTER THREE

Vanessa drove to Scottsdale Community College, where she taught Introductory Italian on Mondays and Wednesdays from 1:00 pm to 3:00 pm and Intermediate Italian on Tuesdays and Thursdays from 12:00 pm until 2:00 pm. She didn't have to work and certainly didn't need the money. The simple fact was that Vanessa simply enjoyed teaching. She was a good instructor and well-liked by her students.

Jake never understood why Vanessa took a job in the first place. If he wore her shoes, and possessed her inheritance, which continually grew due to prudent investments, he wouldn't be practicing law today. Instead, he'd be in Mexico or on a tropical isle soaking up the sun. When she came home from the college late and dinner wouldn't be ready on time, he would lay on the guilt. Of course he applied a double standard when he came home late. No matter what Jake said, Vanessa needed to work because it kept her sane. She wasn't like other wealthy women who could go to spas and luncheons or shop all day. She needed to have a purpose and did so by giving back to the community in numerous ways.

After she got pregnant in her junior year of college, she was forced to drop out a semester, during which she had a miscarriage. Going back to school redirected her mind from the loss of her child. When she told Jake of her decision to complete her education, he looked at her as if she had lost her mind.

"Why would you go back to school? You don't need to, not when you have all the money you'll ever need."

Vanessa smiled. "You don't know who I really am, Jake. I'm not motivated by money—"

"That's because you were raised with it and lacked nothing growing up," he said forcefully.

"Jake, I want to be a useful, person who gives back to society. If I just lived off my money, I'd feel like a parasite."

"Really? Have you forgotten you already give your time and money to a number of charities. Isn't that enough?" But, before Vanessa could reply, Jake said, waving his hand in dismissal, "Never mind. It's *your* money. Do what you like."

"You do realize that I actually don't need your permission," she said with unusual boldness.

Jake glared at her, but said nothing and walked away.

The image faded in her mind as Vanessa parked the car in the faculty lot. Then she headed for the Language and Communications Building where she lectured. She liked to get there early to show that she appreciated promptness. By setting a precedent, she hoped her students would likewise come to class on time.

Today was Monday and it was time for her intro class in Italian, which had an enrollment of 18 students. Vanessa appreciated small classes because she could give more individualized attention to the students.

Vanessa watched as her students entered the classroom. Over the years she discovered there was always one needy student in every class. Denny Moore could be that poster child. If it were possible, he would monopolize all her time during class. This was the second week of the semester and she hoped his needs would lessen, but she now feared that was only wishful thinking. She tried to look busy as he walked into the classroom so he would sit down and not approach her. Her ruse didn't work. He was patiently standing at her desk waiting for her to look up.

"What is it, Denny?" she inquired hoping he would be quick.

He removed his homework from his bag and placed it on the desk in front of her. "I had a great deal of trouble translating the passages."

"We'll be going over it in class and if you still have trouble make an appointment to see me. You know my office hours."

Denny looked at her with his adoring puppy eyes and shook his head. It was then that the bell signaling the start of class rang. Vanessa nodded for him to go sit down. He did so obediently and she was able to start class.

***

Jake was in court presenting to the judge what his client desired in the settlement. The opposing counsel, Brittany Ashwood, was doing the same for her client, but with a slight twist. She was using her feminine wiles in an attempt to sway the judge. She'd already gotten Jake's attention. He half listened as he imagined what it would be like to bed her. The woman was full-breasted and long-legged. Her blonde hair was tied up in a bun and he imagined taking it down and running his fingers through it. She wasn't beautiful in the classic sense, but was attractive enough for a midday romp. The more he thought about it, the more he wanted her.

Olivia Simmons was irked that Jake was paying more attention to the other lawyer than he was to her. True, he was getting her practically everything she wanted to a point, but what she truly wanted was him. What did that other woman have that she didn't? Youth? Overrated and to hell with it. Maturity was where it was at. She knew exactly what it took to pleasure and keep a man.

To an onlooker the scene had to be comical with Jake stealing glances at Brittany and Olivia, with narrowed eyes, glaring at Jake.

The attorney finished and gave him a lingering look as she passed him and she sat down. *Yeah*, he thought, *she wants me too.*

That was all that would be done that day, so Jake decided to go for it. After saying goodbye to his own client, he approached the other attorney. She ended her conversation with her client and turned to face Jake. "You want a word with me?"

"Yes, but I'd like to do it over lunch, if that's all right with you."

Brittany Ashwood had no illusions about Jake's intentions. He'd telegraphed exactly what he wanted with his eyes That was okay with her. She was game. Personally, she wanted to see what was under that fancy suit he was wearing.

"Why not? Perhaps we can shorten court time," Brittany said.

Jake drove to the Kimpton Hotel Palomar Phoenix which boasted the Blue Hound Kitchen where one could enjoy southern comfort food with southwest sizzle. He intended to buy his way into her panties with a terrific lunch. Only Brittany had her own version of what would go down. As Jake drove, Brittany had rested her hand firmly on Jake's thigh, giving it a rub every so often. Underneath the conservative suit and hairstyle, the woman was apparently a free spirit.

The Blue Hound was crowded, but they found two seats at the bar. The bartender handed them two menus and asked what they'd be drinking. Brittany ordered a vodka sour and Jake, a Martini. A waitress approached and asked what they'd be eating.

Brittany pointed to her drink and replied, "This is all I need for now."

"And you, sir?"

"Just the drink for now."

What else could Jake say when Brittany was giving him smoldering looks?

She slipped a hand under the bar and placed it on Jake's thigh. Looking at him, she began to move it around until she found the bulge in his pants. A smile formed on her face when she felt him hardening. He placed his hand on top of hers and whispered into her ear, "Not here. Besides, I thought I was seducing you."

"Perhaps you've met your match."

"Is that a challenge?"

"Take it as you wish," she said, running her tongue across her upper lip.

"Perhaps we should get a room in order to continue this conversation."

"Maybe we should," she agreed."

Now that the gauntlet had been dropped between them, it was game on. They finished their drinks and went into the lobby where Brittany waited for Jake to register for a room. Then they headed over to the elevator bank and took one to the fourth floor. Jake swiped the card in the lock of 412 as Brittany nuzzled his neck. The door barely closed behind them before his lips were on hers. Her lipstick tasted like wild berries. He wondered what the rest of her tasted like. As Jake pushed Brittany up against the closest wall, that kiss led to more feverish ones and it might appear from an onlooker as if they were trying to devour one another.

He fervently kissed her, undoing his slacks and letting them slip down to his thighs, while he lifted her skirt, ripping her silk panties off and slipping inside her. Jake grunted and jack- hammered in and out of Brittany as fast and as hard as he could, causing them both to orgasm quickly. However, neither one was satiated.

Jake kicked off his slacks before carrying Brittany over to the bed. Dropping down nearly on top of her, his lips crushed hers as the rest of their clothes haphazardly flew to the carpet. This time Jake wanted to take his time and explore every inch of Brittany's superb body.

Starting with her plump berry-sweetened lips, which he kissed and bit with a savage intensity, he made his way down, kissing her jaw and neck, slowly descending to linger on her still heaving breasts. He teased and nipped at the twin rosebuds, causing Brittany to mewl and her body to quiver. As Jake swathed each erect nipple with his tongue, his fingers kneaded and fanned the other. Brittany's body bucked and gyrated as her nails clawed his back.

His mouth and lips slid further down until they came to her flat stomach. He swirled his tongue into her navel and discovered that she was ticklish. After tormenting her a few more minutes, he grasped both her hips and spread her legs, before burrowing his head between her thighs.

Jake lathed her labia with the flat of his tongue, but teased her by avoiding contact with her clitoris. Brittany gyrated her body in order to get him to suck it, but he was enjoying her squirming much too much to give in too quickly.

As Brittany neared her climax, she became desperate, pleading with him as she tried to control the movement of Jake's head. When he'd felt he'd tortured her enough, he nipped at her clitoris and almost immediately, she climaxed.

There would be no round three since it was getting late. Jake wanted to get home at a reasonable hour today, especially if Vanessa had gotten home early and was waiting for him. He left Brittany stretched out on the bed as he went into the bathroom to shower. Being quite satisfied, he was hoping that she was as well and wouldn't follow him in. She didn't. In fact, while Jake was showering, Brittany dressed. She left him a note on the hotel stationery. "Thanks for a good time. Had to go home to my little girl."

Perfect, Jake thought reading the note. *All I wanted was a one-night stand.* He went back to the reservation desk and the concierge called a cab to take him back to the courthouse parking lot where he'd left his car.

Getting into the cab, he turned his head in the direction of a car engine starting. A red Cadillac Escalade was pulling out of a parking space and heading for the exit. Olivia Simmons drove an Escalade, he thought, but dismissed the idea of it being hers. He had Olivia Simmons on the brain. Thank God her divorce was nearly finalized and she was history.

***

Denny sat in Vanessa's tiny office as she explained how to conjugate the verbs he hadn't gotten correct. There was definitely a gleam in his gray eyes. Vanessa hoped it was interest in the Italian and not in her. She hated when one of the young men got a crush on her and she had to let them down. Men's egos were fragile, but the egos of young men were worse.

Glancing at her watch, Vanessa saw how late it had gotten and realized she had to wrap things up with Denny and go home. As she watched him struggle with a verb, she became concerned that perhaps she truly couldn't help him. Perhaps he couldn't grasp the work or maybe he needed a better tutor. She knew she couldn't keep giving all her free time to helping him. He'd stopped making appointments to speak to her, merely showing up at her office, and there were others who might need her, as well. She had to find a delicate way to stop his behavior without hurting his feelings. She grappled with this situation for several minutes before coming to a decision.

"Denny, we have to stop now. Obviously, you are not getting this and I have tried every approach I know. So, I suggest you seek out a tutor—"

"No! You're my teacher."

"True, but I'm not helping you. Here is the name—"

"No. I'd rather quit."

"You're taking this all wrong. I think someone new with a fresh approach might be better for you. That's all I'm suggesting," Vanessa replied with some frustration.

But, before Vanessa could say another word, Denny grabbed his things and bolted out her office door. The look on his face caused strings of guilt tying knots around her heart. Unfortunately, she was at a loss not knowing what else could she have done. She'd given him as much time as she could afford and had no other choice. If only she was as decisive with her own husband.

She refused to admit what was so obvious. Jake was more than likely cheating on her. No lawyer worked as many hours as he did. It wasn't as if he had no staff. She knew he had several competent lawyers and a full-time investigator working for him. How naïve did he think she was? Especially when the fluctuation of hours came every so often. He'd tell her it was a big case, but weren't they all? No. Vanessa guessed it was most likely interest in a new woman. She'd been through this before. Or should she say, many times before. Perhaps it *was* time to take some decisive action. She no longer loved him as she once had— or thought she had. One day, she was going to leave him. She'd have to find a good—no better lawyer than Jake. Knowing Jake, no matter what he did, it wasn't going to be easy to divorce him. What a spectacle the divorce might end up being. Was that why she was dragging her feet?

Vanessa finished packing up her books, grabbed her purse and book bag and left her office. Seeing that no other student had been waiting to speak to her, she headed outside the parking lot wondering if Jake will be home for dinner. Cooking dinner for two, only to throw half of it out most of the time was wasteful. And sometimes very lonely.

CHAPTER FOUR

Vanessa had no classes today, so she decided to stop by her friend, Elliot Kastner's law office. Elliott was the present executor of the trust fund set up for Vanessa by her father, Francis Torelli, who was once the Ambassador to Italy and had returned there to live in Rome after her mother died. Originally the fund was administered by Elliot's father, Stephen. When Stephen succumbed to a stroke that took his life, Elliot, a good estate planning attorney in his own right, took over. Funds from the trust had been invested wisely and Vanessa was able to draw from that revenue when she needed money.

Because the Kastners and the Torellis had been close friends and often vacationed together, Elliot and Vanessa saw a great deal of each other growing up. Since neither one of them had any siblings, they considered themselves brother and sister. However, because of this, neither would reveal to the other about their true feelings. The line that separated friend from lover was growing quite thin.

When Vanessa entered his office, Elliot's face brightened and his green eyes twinkled. His auburn hair was neatly trimmed and his blue tailored suit impeccable, but it was his adorable dimples that made her smile. She took a quick look around and noticed that nothing had changed, from the rich mahogany bookcases, comfortable looking chairs and sofa, to the beautiful paintings of the rock formations of Sedona and Antelope Valley.

Elliot rose to greet her, giving her a warm kiss on the cheek. "Hi, how are you? What has it been— two weeks?"

"About that. I missed you, too. Unfortunately, I've been overwhelmed, especially with work. But I'm here now. How's about some lunch?"

"Lunch sounds good. Want to go anyplace special?"

"No. Besides, I think it's your turn to decide on the restaurant. I'm pretty sure I chose the restaurant last time."

"Okay then. I know just the place," Elliot said, heading for the door and holding it for Vanessa.

Elliot drove Vanessa in his silver Genesis Coupe to a small restaurant several blocks away. They were led to a small table by the greeter who left two menus on the table.

"I've eaten here several times, Vanessa. The menu may be limited, but everything I've chosen in the past was good. Their fries and onion rings are homemade and to die for."

"I'm not certain I want to have onion rings as my last meal," she kidded.

Elliot laughed. His laugh was rich and had the power to always draw her in.

"Seriously, I'll have whatever you are with an iced tea," she said. "I'm going to wash my hands."

"Okay, then. Lunch will be a surprise," Elliot said and winked.

Elliot watched Vanessa walk away. He sensed something was bothering her and he had the feeling it had something to do with Jake. Despite her smile he could see the sadness in her eyes. If it were up to him and he had the power, he would wave a magic wand and make every day a sunny one for her. He loved her that much.

The waiter came to take their order and Elliot decided on two grilled chicken salads with iced tea. That was what Vanessa had had for dinner the night that changed his life forever.

He still replayed that one night that they had way too much to drink and had barely made it back to Vanessa's house. He had been in no condition to drive home. Both sets of parents were in Paris on vacation, and the maid had gone home. The house was empty and Vanessa had insisted he remain the night. And Elliot knew he'd never make it home in one piece, so he agreed.

They sat together watching an old movie on the den couch. Apparently the alcohol had dampened Vanessa's inhibitions. She turned to face him and had that come on look that women often got when they were horny. Elliott knew they were friends and having sex would take them over that imaginary line that friends never crossed. He couldn't count how many times he desired to obliterate the line, but hadn't due to their friendship. But that look and the closeness of her body heated his. The desire to kiss her pillowed lips was overwhelming, so he did.

Vanessa kissed him back with such intensity that it got an instant response from his cock. The dam of his desire broke, he covered her mouth hungrily. When she returned his kiss with reckless abandon, he knew there was no turning back.

His hands caressed her breasts through her blouse causing her to moan. As he began to unbutton her blouse, she reached for the zipper on his jeans and freed his erection. She began to stroke him as he suckled and massaged her breasts. Breathlessly, she helped him pull off her jeans.

Elliot kissed her pussy through her silk panties. She twisted her fingers in his hair as her body gyrated with pleasure. "I need to feel you inside me. Please, Elliot."

The feeling that he got as he entered her was one that he'd never forget.

The memory faded as Vanessa returned. She slipped back into the booth and smiled at him.

"So, Vanessa, how are things at home?"

Vanessa sighed.

"Not any better?"

"Not really. Jake's hardly ever home for dinner, says he's working."

"You're not sure?"

Vanessa shook her head. "I have a feeling is having an affair."

Elliot's face hardened. "Damn him. Why can't he treat you better? If you were—" he stopped abruptly realizing what he was about to say and stopped. "He should be more loving and not so cavalier with your love."

Vanessa had moved her hand over Elliot's. "You know I care for you and always will, but unlike my husband, I try to live up to my vows."

Elliott raised an eyebrow. "No matter how hard?"

"Yes. Only it's been even harder lately. I've been entertaining thoughts of leaving him."

Elliot wanted to jump for joy, but not at the expense of her pain. Instead, he said, "So, it's gotten that bad. I'm sorry to hear that."

"I don't intend to be the dutiful, clinging wife that learns to look the other way while he fucks other women."

"Then, what you intend to do, Vanessa?"

"At this point, I'm not certain."

Their food came and Vanessa was pleasantly surprised. When she realized it was a grilled chicken salad, she looked up at Elliot and smiled knowingly. She remembered.

They ate in silence for a few moments. Vanessa knew there was little more to be said about her relationship with Jake at this time, so she changed the subject. "I'm thinking of going to Rome to visit with my dad."

"When?" Elliot forked some salad into his mouth and chased it down with some iced tea.

"During the winter break."

"That's nice. Not having him around must be hard on you."

"You learn to accept it. Then seeing him becomes more wonderful."

Elliott smiled. "You know, I miss him, too."

"Of course you do. We were like one big extended family. I loved those times. They were magical."

"Yes, they were." Elliott glanced at his watch. "I have to be back for an appointment soon, so we have to leave in a few minutes. I'd rather stay here, though."

Vanessa looked into Elliot's beautiful green eyes and smiled. "Me, as well."

***

It was hard for Elliot to keep his mind on the middle-aged man sitting across from him who needed his services as an estate lawyer. Instead, his mind kept replaying Vanessa's words about divorcing Jake.

The very fact that Vanessa had finally admitted her marriage was in shambles and that divorce was most likely on the horizon, gave him hope that they would finally be together. This was what was meant to be. He just knew and felt it beyond the shadow of a doubt. She was his soulmate—the reason he'd been put on this earth.

***

As Vanessa drove home, she thought about Elliot and how much she truly loved him. Even though she said she'd uphold her marriage vows, she wanted to break them and physically love him as well. Just the thought of making love to Elliot sent a warm glow through her. If only Jake had not entered her life.

The memory of her first meeting with Jake cooled the warm glow. She remembered how he'd tried to pick her up in a bar and how she totally disliked him. However, when the friend she'd come with left with some guy, she stayed to finish her drink and actually let him buy her another as they talked. He seemed not so bad after all. When she'd realized that she'd had too much to drink, he'd driven her home. She'd awoken in her own bed with him on the couch with no memory of how she'd gotten there.

They began to date, and when she discovered she was pregnant, they got married. That was the story she'd accepted until she discovered he'd gotten a vasectomy after she lost the baby. Then she began to wonder about the missing memory and the possibility that he'd slipped the date-rape drug, rohypnol, into her drink while she was in the ladies room. Knowing now what she didn't know then, she knew that Jake was capable of doing nearly anything to get what he wanted.

The blare of a car horn snapped Vanessa out of the memory and she drove the rest of the way home with more pleasant thoughts.

CHAPTER FIVE

Vanessa continued to immerse herself with teaching in a vain attempt to forget about her failing marriage and the missed opportunity with Elliot. She recieved an invitation from the Children's Hospital, her pet charity. Despite Jake's cynicism, she felt comfort in knowing her donations of time and money went to helping sick children.

There was going to be a black-tie dinner to honor Dr. Lutz, the head of the pediatric wing, who was retiring. Vanessa liked the short, rotund man with unruly steely-gray hair that reminded her of Albert Einstein. Wanting to wish him well, she intended to attend. She'd mention it to Jake when he came home from work. Perhaps he'd agree to accompany her.

***

Jake came home on time. His mood was light and dinner was an enjoyable one. He amused Vanessa with the antics of a divorcing couple and how they fought tooth and nail over everything, including their pets, which was quite a menagerie.

After Jake had finished, Vanessa told him about the invitation to the black-tie dinner.

"You know how I feel about those ridiculous parties." Jake replied, his demeanor turning icy.

"Yes, but this is very important to me. Besides, I'm tired of attending all my special occasions alone."

"If it's a warm body that you need, why don't you take your friend, Elliot Kastner. Maybe he's free for the evening."

"But, you're my husband. I should attend with you, not a surrogate," Vanessa protested.

"Yes, but I have no desire to attend and he'll make an excellent stand-in for me. After all, you're such good friends and will find something to talk about."

Really, Jake? He'll make more of a replacement for you.

***

Elliot thought about the implications of Vanessa's asking him to accompany her to a black-tie event. The first question that came to mind was why wasn't Jake attending with her?

He knew that Vanessa wasn't happy with Jake at times, but wondered if things had soured to a new low. This bothered him. As much as he loved her, he didn't wish unhappiness on Vanessa. And yet, he'd hoped all these years for her to leave Jake and finally become his.

Elliot remembered when the blush first faded from Vanessa's marriage. It had been nearly two years after losing her baby that she mentioned her inability to have any more children. Of course, Elliot had asked if she'd gone to a fertility doctor for answers. He remembered her reply. "Jake said they shouldn't bother. He already had fathered a child. Therefore, it was obvious that the problem had to lie with her. If they were meant to have children, she would have become pregnant again. I guess I have to agree with him."

This was what Vanessa thought and accepted until they met one of Jake's old buddies from his first law firm for dinner. The guy seemed nice enough until he began to complain about how fertile his wife was. They already had two children and she was pregnant again. When Jake suggested that the man do what he'd done—get a vasectomy, there would be no more crying infants to contend with. Vanessa realized that Jake had forgotten she was sitting at the table. Nothing more was said about the vasectomy and the fact that Jake had been so untruthful until they left the restaurant. She couldn't hold her tongue any longer and confronted him in the car. They argued all the way home. What was worse, Vanessa knew she'd never be able to forgive Jake for what he'd done. His deceit was the worst thing he'd ever done to her.

Elliot remembered how hurt Vanessa had been. She'd wanted children so much and to be so deceived by Jake simply broke her heart. She never got over it. Now, four years later, she appeared to be done. He guessed there were things a person could not get over no matter how they tried.

***

Elliot picked Vanessa up. She met him at the door and didn't ask him in. Jake was in his office and she didn't want him to come out and say something stupid with the intent of spoiling the evening.

As they walked toward Elliot's silver Genesis, he said, "Van, you look simply gorgeous tonight."

"Why thank you. You know I could say the same about you. That suit fits you like a glove."

"That's what happens when you miss the gym three times in one week," Elliot replied with laughter in his voice.

Vanessa laughed. She adored his quick wit which always put her in a good mood.

They drove to the Children's Hospital talking about the people who would definitely be there and those who might come. Vanessa felt this was small talk was and not what she needed. What she wanted to talk about concerned him and her. All she thought about lately was the colossal mistake she'd made in marrying Jake.

Jake hardly touched her anymore. Ironically, she really didn't care. He seemed too full of himself and his own needs. And when he did make love to her, she didn't feel engaged. It was if her body responded to his touch, because she needed to be touched and held, but emotionally she was with Elliot.

She tried to remember when this became the norm. It just didn't happen. It was like a slow cancer, mestastising. She wondered if she should tell Elliot. Was it the right time or not? She wasn't certain.

They arrived at the hospital. The valet took Elliot's car and they ventured inside to greet the hospital administrator and the various department heads. Elliott steered her toward the drinks and hors d'oeuvres. He'd rather be alone with her and not have to share her with anyone.

When the band began to play a slow ballad, Elliot asked Vanessa if she'd like to dance.

The thought of being in Elliot's arms delighted her. "I'd love to, Elliot," Vanessa said, taking his hand in hers.

She melted into his arms and he placed his hand firmly around her waist in a possessive gesture. They began to move slowly gliding along the polished wooden floor. Vanessa felt secure in Elliot's arms and all the old feelings came fluttering back like softly falling rose petals. She wished she could remain in Elliot's arms forever. If only she hadn't fallen for Jake's scheming....*Stop it!* She demanded of herself. *Do not spoil this wonderful evening with thoughts of Jake.* Her time with Elliot was fleeting. She should try to make the best of it.

Vanessa knew that Elliot would never compromise her reputation at a public gathering. Just once, how she wished he would hold her close and nuzzle her neck. And how she wanted their hearts so close they could beat as one. Dancing with Elliott was so pleasurable that it was pure torture. His closeness was heavenly, but unfortunately temporary and therefore masochistic. Still, Vanessa didn't care. She longed to run her fingers through Elliot's hair. Any such move would definitely raise eyebrows and end up on the gossip columns in the local news. Even so, she nearly dared. The song ended way too soon. Elliott smiled down at Vanessa and led her off the dance floor. She wished she could have remained in his arms just a little longer. It was torture to leave them.

Vanessa adored everything about Elliot from his wit to his tenderness. He had a softer approach to life than Jake and was still somewhat idealistic, even for an estate lawyer. He didn't just go through the motions. He still cared for others and tried to do the best for them. He never looked at Vanessa as a financial gain, though she was nearly certain that Jake did. Sometimes she felt that was the reason he married her. Perhaps he thought he'd eventually get her money.

Elliot's eyes studied Vanessa with curious intensity. "Earth to Vanessa," he said. "Where are you?"

"Oh, I'm so sorry, Elliot. I was lost in thought."

"I hope it was about me."

Vanessa gave Elliot a cryptic smile which he could interpret anyway he'd like.

Another slow song began to play and they got up to dance again. Vanessa closed her eyes and luxuriated in Elliot's closeness.

***

Vanessa and Elliot left before the party ended. She needed to make a showing and she did. She said goodbye and wished Dr. Lutz her best. She just found it difficult to remain much longer. There was so much snobbery that a person could take in one room. The rich never seemed to be quiet about their money. They wore flashy clothes and expensive jewelry as they spoke glowingly about their investments in numerous homes and other acquisitions. She had never wanted to become one of them. It was good to have financial freedom, but to flaunt it was just not her style.

The valet brought the car and they got inside. Elliot pulled out of the parking lot and parked. Turning to face Vanessa, he asked, "Ae you tired or would you like to stop somewhere quiet for a drink?"

The longer Vanessa was with Elliot, the happier she was. "I'm fine with stopping somewhere."

Elliot thought a moment. "I know just the place," he said and pulled back into traffic.

They drove for several minutes before he pulled into a parking lot of a small bar.

"There's not a car here," Vanessa said. "Maybe the place is closed."

Sure enough, there was a sign on the door. Closed for renovations.

"Shall we try another place?" Vanessa asked.

"My condo is only a few miles away. If I promise to behave, we can go there. My bar is fully stocked."

Vanessa was torn. That was exactly where she wanted to go, however, she had to be more honorable than Jake— not that she cared to be one iota. She wanted to forget she was married to the man.

"I have a pitcher of Margaritas," Elliot added to sweeten the pot.

"You drive a hard bargain."

"So we're off to my place, then?"

"Uh-huh,"

"Don't be so excited about it," Elliot said, grinning.

If only you knew how I truly felt.

They sat side-by-side on Elliot's terrace facing the Camelback Mountains, sipping Margaritas. The mountains were a purple haze against the black night sky filled with dazzling stars. Only the cooing of doves could be heard. The night air was crisp, but not chilly enough to use the propane heater.

"It's such a lovely night," Vanessa said, as she sipped her drink.

"Not as lovely as you," Elliot said.

Vanessa smiled warmly at him. "You're always there to make me feel wonderful."

"No matter what, I always will," he said, leaning over to kiss her cheek. But Vanessa turned to face toward him at the same time allowing their lips to meet.

It was a chaste kiss between friends until their eyes locked. Then that one kiss became a flurry of kisses. Vanessa fell backward on the couch and Elliot covered her body with his. Instinct took over and the velvet night turned to gold.

A beat later, Elliot slipped his hand under Vanessa's dress. He then pulled her panties down and off as Vanessa worked on the zipper of his slacks. She moaned softly as he slipped inside, filling her. "Oh, Vanessa," he half-whispered, half-groaned. "How I've wanted this for so long."

They moved as one quickly, hurtling toward their peaks, reaching their orgasms nearly simultaneously. It was quick, but sweet. And not nearly enough to sate either of them. After several minutes of rest, they went inside up to Elliot's bedroom to make love again, only this time more leisurely. As they slowly undressed one another, they took the time to savor every kiss, every gentle touch and sweet feeling.

As Vanessa ran her fingers through Elliot's hair and over the muscles of his hard back, he fondled one soft mound and used his tongue and lips to tease the erect tip of the other breast. He tantalized both buds for several minutes before his hand seared a path down her abdomen and onto her thigh. His touch was light and painfully teasing, especially when he moved to the inside of her thigh.

His lips followed his hands, tracing a sensuous path to pleasure and Vanessa moaned loudly. Elliot tongued Vanessa's sex with long, deliberate strokes from top to bottom causing Vanessa's body to twitch. When he began to shift his attention to her clitoris, her moaning grew louder until her entire body began to gyrate. As Elliot continued to please Vanessa, her moans lasted longer until she cried out as the first undulations of her orgasm rolled over her like a tidal wave.

When she was finished, she grabbed for his cock and guided it inside of her. As their lips came together, their bodies began to move measuredly, searching for their special rhythm. Once they obtained it, Elliot began to plunge deeper and faster until he cried out and exploded inside her. Both were now thoroughly sated and they held each other close.

They fell asleep in one another's arms and awoke around 2:30 am. After showering together, Elliot drove Vanessa home. It was nearly 4:30 am and the house was dark.

"Do you think that Jake waited up for you?"

Vanessa shrugged. "What difference does it make? He hasn't touched me in a long time. Besides, I'm in love with you, Elliot," she said, placing a finger on his lips. "Let me finish. I've wanted to tell you this for ages. I've loved you for forever and now know that my marriage to Jake was so wrong on too many levels to mention."

"You have no idea how long I've waited to hear those words from you," Elliot said, cupping Vanessa's chin and drawing his face close to hers. I'm thrilled that tonight happened, but if you feel any guilt come tomorrow, I'm okay with that, because I understand."

Their lips met in a tender kiss. Vanessa's heart swelled with the love she felt for Elliot. When their lips parted, she wished him a good night and let herself out of the car. Elliot watched as she entered the house before pulling away.

There wasn't a light on in the house and it was still. Vanessa flipped on the hall lights and started up the steps. There was a small nightlight in the hall outside the master bedroom. The door was open and she could see that the bed was still made. Jake was elsewhere.

Vanessa's eyes narrowed. Where could he be at this hour. She realized it was calling the kettle black, but wouldn't it have been prudent of him to get home before she did?

She heard the key in the lock and the front door opening. Gritting her teeth, she went to greet him.

"Oh, Vanessa, didn't expect to see you standing there at this hour."

"That's fairly obvious. Late hours at the office?" she said sarcastically.

Jake chuckled. "Of course not. I went out with some friends and had a little car trouble, but no worries, It got fixed and here I am."

Vanessa thought she detected a hint of perfume, but didn't want to ruin the wonderful evening she'd had with Elliot by arguing with Jake. Instead of confronting him, she merely said, "Glad you're home safely. I'm going to bed. Good night."

She walked away, leaving Jake standing there looking after her.

CHAPTER SIX

Vanessa did a great deal of soul-searching about her life and where she wanted to be since that beautiful night of Dr. Lutz's retirement party. It was time to divorce Jake. And if she intended to do so, she wanted to make certain her finances were protected. She had called to make an appointment with Elliot, since this visit with him would be strictly business.

"How can I help you this morning, Vanessa?" Elliot asked as he greeted her.

"When we last spoke, I told you things weren't good between Jake and me. Well, they haven't improved much and we're very much like two ships passing on the water. He comes and I go. Not much of a marriage if you ask me."

"If I helped push you to this point, I'm sorry."

"Elliot, I'm glad about what happened between us. You have nothing to feel sorry for," Vanessa said as she reached across his desk to pat his hand. What I need from you today is assurances that Jake won't be able to touch my trust fund. He makes enough money in his own right."

"Understood. I'll draw up the papers to change the beneficiary. A new will is in order, as well. Then you'll need a divorce lawyer who can stand up to Jake. I'll ask around and see who's available and get back to you on that."

"Do you really think he'd take his own case, Elliot?"

"Why not, he's the best of the best. Are you still going to see your dad during the Christmas break?"

"Most definitely. I haven't seen him for such a long time. Besides, I need to discuss my intentions to divorce Jake. He'll be thrilled."

"Really?" Elliot's eyebrows rose in surprise.

"Oh, yeah. He never wanted me to marry him. He said he was shady."

"Wow. I did not know that."

"I had to wage a campaign for Jake in order to get my dad to accept him."

"Well, your dad is a real gentleman. I doubt he'll tell you I told you so."

"Probably not," Vanessa said, "but it is what it is."

She stayed just a little while longer before saying goodbye.

***

Vanessa decided it was best not to argue with Jake over his crazy hours. She wanted him to think that everything was fine and then hit him with the fact she was filing for divorce. Then it will have the effect of being hit between the eyes with a two by four. Even so, he had a special knack for pushing her buttons, and despite her attempts at restraint, they got into a spat over the dinner she left him heating in the oven. By the time he came home, the meat tasted like crap and had the consistency of shoe leather.

"You come home nearly five hours late and you expect your dinner, which had been made hours before, to be perfect? I don't think so."

"If you cared about me, it would be. I know plenty of wives who make it so."

"Yes, I bet you do, but aren't they your clients who are now divorced?"

"Damn it! You have an answer for everything! You know what? Forget it. Keep your shitty dinner. I'm out of here."

Vanessa watched him walk out of the kitchen, grab his jacket and leave. She collapsed into a kitchen chair. *What the hell was wrong with that man?*

***

Cheryl Pratt was not a fool. She was willing to wait a reasonable amount of time for Jake to divorce his wife. However, that time had past. Even though Jake was paying the rent on the condo and giving her spending money, he didn't come around as often as he once had. She began to wonder if she'd lost favor with him and he'd found someone else and would soon replace her. That, coupled with the fact she enjoyed sex, brought her to the brink.

She decided that if Jake didn't call that evening, she'd go out and find a boy toy to fuck her. In the meantime, she needed to relax. Cheryl decided that a soak in a bubble bath might do the trick. She turned on the water and poured in a capful of jasmine scented bubbles. Then she went into the kitchen for a glass of wine. As the tub filled, she undressed and sipped the wine. She slipped into the tub and closed her eyes, imagining Jake was there with her. Cheryl placed the glass down on the side of the tub and picked up a washcloth. She unhurriedly ran it down her full breasts, watching as her nipples grew hard and erect, imagining Jakes lips on them, alternately tugging and sucking. Moaning softly, she imagined Jake moving the cloth down her body, over her flat belly and between her legs. Jake rubbed her clit, sending one wave of pleasure after another throughout her body. Cheryl inserted two fingers into her snatch and began to finger-fuck herself, imagining that Jake had replaced the cloth with his tongue and was flicking his tongue in and out of her, before wrapping his talented tongue around her erect clit, bringing her close to an orgasm. She moved her fingers faster and faster as she pinched one of her nipples until she was drowned in a sea of self-gratification. When her orgasm subsided, Cheryl realized the water had gotten cold. Reaching for a towel, she got out of the tub and toweled herself dry.

***

Cheryl's patience finally gave out at nine. She put on a slinky, short red dress and matching six-inch heels. After one last look at her makeup, she drove to a hangout for college kids in Tempe. She was in the mood to get laid by a young and energetic guy.

It took all of ten minutes, from the time the tall, good-looking, dark-haired lanky guy approached her and offered to buy her a drink, to the time he agreed to follow her to her place. Their conversation had been short and to the point.

"I have a well-stocked bar at my place and some weed. Wanna come for a nightcap you'll never forget?"

The guy shrugged. "Sure."

"Let's go. You can follow me."

Cheryl had become so horny that she rubbed herself during the drive back to the condo. She couldn't wait to get the guy naked and feel his skin against hers.

***

When Jake let himself into Cheryl's condo, he found the downstairs dark. He smiled as he headed up the carpeted stairs, hoping to find her exactly where he wanted her—in bed. Oh, he found her in bed, all right. Unfortunately, she wasn't alone. If Vanessa had stoked the coals, Cheryl poured gasoline on them.

Like a bull seeing red, Jake barged inside the bedroom and confronted Cheryl. The young stud she was with jumped off the bed and covered his deflating genitals as he searched frantically for his pants.

Cheryl knew Jake was furious by his stone-cold glare lasering on her. She tried to do what she did best, use her sexual charms to mollify him.

"Oh, baby, am I glad to see you," she said as he came nearer.

"Really. Then explain to me who that piece of shit was you were fucking and what he was doing in our bed," he spat, pointing to the guy who was about to flee the room.

"You of all people should know that I'm a passionate woman with needs. I felt I was being neglected for so long, that I thought I was going to be replaced by someone new."

"For God's sake! It was what, a week? Week-and-a-half?" He opened and closed his fists.

Watching his hands made her nervous. "It was just about sex. I love only you," she whined.

"Pack your things and get out before I strangle you."

"But I need some time to find another place to live."

"Be gone by tomorrow night, or I'll have you arrested for breaking and entry as well as trespass."

Jake stormed out of the condo. Whatever sexual desires he'd come with had been snuffed out like a candle and yet he had no desire to return home to Vanessa. Sleeping on the couch in his office was more desirable than sleeping in her bed.

Cheryl knew there was no way she'd be able to calm Jake down to the point where she could change his mind. The best course of action would be for her to clear out for now and find temporary housing. Jake might be angry with her tonight, but tomorrow was a new day.

CHAPTER SEVEN

Between the problem with Denny, the needy student who eventually dropped her class, and the seemingly growing distance between her and Jake, Vanessa thought the winter break at college would be a good time to visit her father. Since he'd moved to Rome, she wasn't able to see very much of him. Being the former Ambassador to Rome from the United States for eight years, he'd grown to love the people and their country, vowing to return to live one day. Ambassador Torelli kept his word following the death of his wife from ovarian cancer.

The winter break, which was still a few weeks away, would give Vanessa two weeks to spend with her father, who lived in a lovely apartment on the via Del Corso, one of the main shopping streets in Rome. Vanessa had been there once before and it had reminded her of the French quarter in New Orleans.

Vanessa asked Jake to come with her, but he said there were too many cases that were drawing to a close that needed his attention. So he told her to go and enjoy herself, which was what she intended. She'd only asked Jake to be polite. She hadn't expected him to accept her invitation.

A week before Vanessa was to leave for Rome, she received a call from the local police in Rome. Though the man who called her spoke heavily accented English, Vanessa was able to understand that her father had been run down as he crossed the street by a drunk driver.

"Is he okay?" Vanessa asked hopefully.

"No, no, no, signora. He is dead. Sorry for your loss."

"When can I come to retrieve his body? I want to bury him in the United States."

"As soon as the autopsy is done. Then you can come to the morgue and make arrangements to transport the body."

Vanessa jotted down the address of the morgue and hung up. Her tears were cascading down her cheeks as she dialed Elliot's number. Jake was out somewhere and she didn't know who else to call.

Elliot answered on the second ring. Noting it was Vanessa, he asked, "Everything okay?"

Vanessa sighed heavily as she tearfully replied, "Elliot, nothing is right. My father's dead—"

"What! How is that possible? He was such a robust man."

"He wasn't sick. My father was killed by a drunk driver. It was a hit-and-run, but they caught him."

Elliot could hear the sobbing in her voice. He wanted to console her. "Oh, Vanessa, I'm so sorry. I'll be right over."

"No. You don't have to come. Jake should be home soon. Just wanted you to know."

"Will you have him buried in the States or in Rome?"

"I think he'd want to be buried next to my mother so I'm going to bring him home."

"When are you flying to Rome?" Elliot asked.

"I hope to take the first available flight tomorrow." Vanessa dabbed at a tear and blew her nose.

"Is Jake going with you?"

Vanessa heard the concern in his voice. "I haven't told Jake yet. You're the only person who knows."

"Would you like me to come with you?"

"Not necessary. I'll be fine. Thanks for offering," Vanessa said.

"I'd like to go. You know how I felt about your dad. He was like another father to me," Elliot reminded her.

Vanessa began to sob audibly. "I know and I'd love you to come with me, but I have to do this myself. With Jake not going, if you came along, it wouldn't look too kosher. I've got to get off now and call the funeral home. I'll call you when I arrive in Rome."

"Be careful, Vanessa. Have a safe trip. If you change your mind, let me know."

With tears clouding her eyes and voice, Vanessa said, "Thank you, Elliot."

FOR THE LOVE OF MONEY

***

The evening news came on as Sofia Ricci was preparing her dinner. Her feet were killing her and she really needed to soak them. Standing on them all day, waitressing, was beginning to take its toll. If the tips weren't so good, she'd look for a different kind of job. Being single, she had to provide for her own room and board. Finding a decent man with a steady job was not as easy as she'd like it to be.

"On the local scene, the former ambassador to Italy from the United States, Francis Torelli, was run down in front of the Nike store on the via Del Corso. He is survived by his daughter, Vanessa Jeffers." A picture of Vanessa Jeffers filled the TV screen. Sofia's heart nearly stopped.

The woman on the screen looks so much like Sofia that she could have been her twin. She paused. Twin? Could that woman be her twin? It was plausible since Sofia had been adopted as an infant. Her real parents had been killed during the terrorist attack at the Leonardo da Vinci Airport in 1985. Her mother had lived long enough for her to be born. What if there were two babies that had survived?

On impulse, Sofia grabbed her android tablet from her purse and Googled Vanessa Jeffers. Vanessa Jeffers had been born the same month in 1985 as she. It couldn't be just a coincidence. She had found her twin. And she was very rich.

As Sofia skimmed through the material listed about Vanessa Jeffers, she realized that in addition to having been adopted by very wealthy people, her twin was also a very accomplished woman. A pang of anger pierced Sofia. Her twin had gotten everything in life easily, while Sofia struggled just to keep a roof over her head and food on the table. Her parents were good people, but they had minimum-wage jobs and worked themselves into early graves. Sofia ended up with very little because of a quirk of fate. Things would've been quite different for her had she been adopted by the ambassador and his wife.

From what she read about Vanessa Jeffers, Sofia perceived that her twin was genuinely a good person who gave back to her community and even worked as a professor despite the fact she was wealthy and could laze around drinking cocktails by a pool all day. Perhaps Vanessa would be kind enough to help Sofia financially. Maybe Sofia could open up her own restaurant. She had nothing to lose and everything to gain. It was definitely time for vacation in Arizona. And why not? Sofia had never been to the United States. It could turn out to be a lot of fun meeting up with her twin sister. All she had to do was secure a small loan to afford the trip.

CHAPTER EIGHT

Vanessa's time in Rome was a blur. She was moving more like a robot than a human. She cleared out her father's two-bedroom apartment and donated all of his clothes to charity. The personal effects that she wanted to keep were packed away in a box. When she was ready to come home, she texted Jake with her itinerary, even though she knew she couldn't depend on him to pick her up at the airport. Mercifully, she slept most of the plane ride home and didn't have to think about her loss.

When a tear-stained Vanessa arrived at the Sky Harbor Airport with the coffin of her father in the cargo bay of the plane, she hadn't expected to see Jake waiting for her at the luggage carousel.

"Jake! I didn't expect to see you here," Vanessa said, her astonishment evident in her voice.

"I know I've been working crazy hours lately making you feel neglected, but being here to give you support is much more important."

Really? Suddenly you're here for me? "Thank you, Jake. I appreciate your coming to pick me up.."

Jake smiled. Then he drew Vanessa into his arms and hugged her to him. She didn't stiffen, but sagged in his arms. She needed comfort and he provided it. "It's going to be all right. I'm here now and always will be here for you."

Vanessa was comforted by his words, hopeful that he was sincere. Then again, she didn't want to dwell on that. What took center stage for her was her father's funeral. He had been a good man and deserved a nice one.

The bell rang, indicating that the luggage would begin shooting out of the chute momentarily.

"How many bags are we waiting for?" Jake asked.

"None. I brought only an overnight bag, but there are two boxes filled with some of my father's things."

They waited for the boxes to appear. Jake grabbed one and then reached for the other. Together they made their way out of the baggage area and headed to the parking lot where Jake had parked the car. Exhausted, Vanessa fell asleep as soon as she sat down in his car and slept most of the way home. When they reached the house, Vanessa stirred and walked into the house and went straight to bed.

*****

The following day, Jake accompanied Vanessa to the funeral home. She picked out a casket and made the final preparations for the funeral which was to be held mid-morning the following day. There would be many dignitaries and friends of her father there and yet, she felt so empty. Realizing that she never had the chance to say goodbye to her father saddened her. And knowing that he was looking forward to her visit broke her heart.

In the car returning home, flashbacks of falling off her bicycle and her father picking her up and putting a bandage on her cut knee, feeling like a princess dancing on the tops of her father's shoes at some gala when she was seven and that special daughter-father dance at her wedding. These thoughts chocked her with such emotion that she couldn't contain her tears.

Jake reached over and patted her thigh. "The pain will lessen over time. You'll see."

Vanessa only wiped away her tears and looked out the passenger window. *Easy for him to say. It wasn't his father.* But, she was emotionally drained. Her first thought was that Jake might intend to turn this situation to his advantage, and yet, it didn't worry her. Instead, she was glad he was acting as a husband should. She needed comfort not confrontation. Had her absence caused him to reflect on their marriage? Perhaps, but she wouldn't bet on it. His track record says differently. She closed her eyes and drifted off.

*****

Jake pulled into their driveway and Vanessa got out and went directly upstairs to their bedroom to lie down. He came upstairs to check on Vanessa and found her sitting on the edge of the bed staring down at the carpet.

He sat down next to her and put his arm around her shoulders. "Your father will always be with you in your heart and head. Nothing can erase that."

Vanessa placed her head on his shoulder. Jake began to gently stroke her face. It felt good to be touched by a slow hand. She couldn't remember the last time he'd been tender with her and basked in his attention,

Jake's lips dropped to her neck. He planted tender kisses causing Vanessa to sigh and close her eyes, delighting in the sensual pleasure. He continued to nuzzle her neck as he slowly opened the buttons on her blouse, kissing the bare skin. His hands slipped under her bra and teased her hard nipples. Vanessa, wanting to feel his mouth on her breasts, unhooked the bra.

He feasted on her bare nipples alternately lathing and tugging them. Vanessa emitted a soft moan. This encouraged Jake, whose lips began to travel down her body, causing it to quiver. A fire surged through her veins, as her heart sang with delight. She hadn't been touched by Jake like this for months.

"I want you naked," Jake said, continuing to undress Vanessa. When she was totally nude, his eyes devoured her. This excited her even further and she wanted to touch Jake, as well. She reached for his erection stretching the front of his jeans, but he swatted her hand away.

"Not yet. I want to pleasure you first."

Good to his word, Jake spent several minutes covering Vanessa's body with soft feathery kisses, making his way down her body to her shapely thighs. She jumped with skittish pleasure as he licked the inside of her right thigh. Coupled with the anticipation of what was to come, she feared drowning in her own juices. And Jake did not disappoint.

Jake moved in between her legs, separating and lifting them, so he could center in on her already wet pussy. Using his tongue he lathed the opening from top to bottom. Vanessa began to tingle inside. Jake nipped and tugged at her clit, which drove her pleasure up to a new level, judging by her staccato breaths and audible moans.

Vanessa knew her climax was fast approaching and wanted Jake to continue doing what he was precisely then, so she held his head down. A beat later, the first wave of her orgasm began to build. As it grew, Vanessa whipped her head from side-to-side on the pillow, never easing up on the pressure she applied to his head. She knew it would be a moment or two before she rode a full-blown wave of ecstasy to heaven.

Finally, with a most vocal cross between a groan, moan, and a scream, Vanessa came. It was several minutes later before the last spasm wracked her body. When she regained her breath, she reached over and began to help Jake undress. She couldn't remember the last time she'd seen her husband in the buff and took a moment to admire his lean athletic body with his long, muscular legs. And as Jake felt her gaze on his body, his erection grew to an appreciable size.

Vanessa guided Jake's cock into her well-lubricated sex. Moving slowly at first, Jake soon began to thrust into her at breakneck speed. At this rate, it took very little time for him to come.

Whatever strength Vanessa had was sapped by the sex and she fell asleep minutes after Jake climaxed. He was far from tired and got out of bed. Suddenly famished, he padded his way down the steps to the kitchen for a snack. He mentally patted his own back for being such a dutiful husband. Servicing Vanessa hadn't cramped his style. His mind was already on the woman he'd met the other day at the coffee shop near Family Court. He smiled at how easy it had been to get her telephone number. The next night, he took her to dinner and was welcomed into her bed afterwards.

CHAPTER NINE

Vanessa pulled on her bathrobe and went downstairs for something to eat. Jake had already left the house for work. She made herself coffee and a muffin and sat down on a barstool at the kitchen breakfast bar. It had been several days since her father's funeral and everything was one big blur in her mind. The funeral had been held at St. Bernard of Claivaux Roman Catholic Church. The pastor had been a close friend of her father's. The pews in the nave were completely filled. The people who couldn't find a seat in the church waited outside to pay their respects. Her father's mahogany coffin was closed. Vanessa couldn't bear to see her father made up like some clown. She wanted to remember him as he was in life.

Following the funeral mass, he was buried next to her mother in Holy Redeemer Catholic Cemetery facing the mountains that he'd loved. Afterwards, there was a catered spread for those who wanted to come back to her home. Jake had hired a waitstaff and had seen to all the details. The sedatives that Vanessa had taken knocked her for a loop so she retired to her bedroom and slept until the following morning.

Elliot had come back to the house wanting to be of some help, but Jake told him that everything was under control and that he should relax and partake of the food. He hated the smug man for all the hurtful things he'd done to Vanessa, but being a gentleman, held his tongue. After having watched Vanessa cling to Jake the entire funeral, it was quite obvious that there had been some reconciliation between them. Normally he'd be happy for her, if that's what she desired, but with Jake's track record, he doubted it would last.

Elliot's heart was breaking just being there while this so-called reconciliation was going on. Therefore he had something to eat and left shortly afterward. He'd check in on Vanessa tomorrow.

***

By the end of one whole week, Jake grew bored of being the perfect husband tending to his distraught wife. His sexual appetite needed to be fed. Since the Cheryl episode, he didn't want to go the mistress route. A harem was more to his liking and he longed to have a stable of women to satisfy his needs. Therefore, he kept the condo for his trysts.

Once again, Jake began to work his so called "late work hours." Vanessa had liked having him around and his attention had been appreciated, but whatever reconciliation she'd thought had taken place had simply disappeared.

Elliot called and asked if she'd like to have lunch. She was ready to rejoin the world. She'd never stop missing her father, but she knew he'd certainly want her to get on with her life. And get on with her life was what she intended to do. She had believed in Jake and given him countless chances. He blew them all. She was so done with him. What she wanted now was a fresh start and knowing how Elliot felt about her was key.

She met Elliot outside a small coffee shop in Phoenix. It was a lovely sunny day in the high seventies so they had coffee and sandwiches at one of the outside tables.

After they ordered, Elliot took one of Vanessa's hands in his. "How are you really doing, Van," he asked.

Vanessa bit her bottom lip. "Emotionally exhausted, but I'm going to live. I'm going to be the kind of woman my father would have wanted me to be."

"But, you already are. You're charitable and kind and—"

"Maybe I'm not explaining it correctly. My father hated Jake. He never just came out and said it, but I knew he only tolerated him because of me. He never wanted me to marry him. I did because of the baby. Oh, sure, I thought I cared for him, but all he showed me was a façade. Underneath the icing is a rotten cake."

"What are you trying to tell me, Van?"

"I'm leaving Jake just as soon as I can get my affairs in order. I don't want him to be able to touch a penny of my trust—not that he needs to, but you know Jake, he could never have enough money."

"That I can tend to asap. When you mentioned this to me the first time, I had all the paperwork drawn up. All I need is your signature."

The waiter brought their sandwiches and refilled their coffees before going back inside.

"Good, because I think Jake won't appreciate me divorcing him. In fact, I think he will take it quite badly and fight me anyway he can."

"I think I've found a good lawyer to whip his ass."

Vanessa giggled. "You know how funny that just sounded?"

"Judging from your reaction, yeah."

She placed her hand on his. "Thank you, Elliot."

"You do realize that I have an ulterior motive don't you?"

Vanessa looked at Elliot questioningly.

"When you divorce is final, I intend to marry you, that is if you'll have me."

A soft smile spread across Vanessa's beautiful face. "I can't wait for the day."

CHAPTER TEN

As Sofia drove from the car rental to Fountain Hills, a distance of about 26 miles according to the GPS in the Toyota Corolla, she appreciated the excellent highways in Arizona. They were far better than the roads back in Italy. She took a sip of the water she'd gotten back at the car rental. This area was so damn dry and warmer than she was used to in December. She could just imagine what the summers were like. It might take some time for her to get used to the dry heat.

According to the GPS, it would take her a little more than a half-hour to reach N. Tabletop Trail, where her twin, Vanessa, lived. Sofia wasn't certain what she would say to her twin when she met her, but if Vanessa was half as nice as she appeared to be, what would it matter? She'd probably be just as excited to meet Sofia—or at least she hoped. A kernel of a plan had formed in the back of Sofia's mind. She'd tell Vanessa how difficult it was to live in Rome and how it was affecting her health. Surely her twin would take pity on her, offering to help.

She turned into the street and drove for another two tenths of a mile, finally coming around the curve when the voice of the GPS told her she'd arrived. Vanessa Jeffers's house was built into the rise of a mountain. It was a two-story, sprawling stucco and stone beauty that made Sofia gasp. "Good Lord!" *My entire apartment in Italy could probably fit into one of the bathrooms,* she thought.

Sofia pulled into the driveway and shut off the car's engine. She sat there just staring out of the window at the house several minutes before getting out. The desert landscaping was lovely. She noticed a working fountain and a pond filled with Koi. Curiosity drove her to see the entire property, so she walked towards the back of the house. A large pool and cabana dominated the rear with several strategically placed fire pits and a hot tub. A stone-built barbecue pit presided at the side of a free-form, stone patio.

She'd seen enough and headed back to the front door. To say she felt cheated was an understatement. From what she learned about Vanessa, not only was she wealthy in her own right, but she was married to the number one divorce lawyer in Arizona. The money that Vanessa was donating to charities could be put to better use by giving it to her. Sofia was positive that she'd be able to put the money to better use.

Sofia stood in front of two ornate wrought iron security doors and depressed the doorbell twice. When no one appeared, she pressed the doorbell again. A beat later, a door flew open, startling her, and a handsome man with an annoyed expression said, "What did you forget and why didn't you use your key?"

It took a few moments for Sofia to realize that he mistook her for Vanessa. "I'm not Vanessa, I'm—"

"Is this is some kind of a joke? And what's with the accent? Save it for your classes."

"Stop talking a moment so I can explain," Sofia said sharply.

Hearing her tone, Jake shut up.

"I'm trying to tell you that I am not your wife. My name is Sofia and I have come from Rome to see Vanessa."

Jake narrowed his eyes looking at Sofia intensely. The woman standing before him could be his wife's identical twin. Was that who she was? His mind raced. Vanessa had been adopted as an infant. Her mother hadn't survived childbirth. This much she knew. He needed answers and would get them if he stopped attacking everything the woman said. "Okay, come inside and tell me *exactly* who you are and what you want."

***

Vanessa wasn't feeling well and left after her class instead of going to her office and being accessible to her students should they need to speak to her. She gathered her papers and placed them into her messenger bag, took her purse from her desk drawer, and headed out the door for her car.

Traffic was heavy and she cursed it. Her head was pounding and she needed to lie down. Gritting her teeth, she endured. As she turned onto N. Tabletop Trail, a dark-blue Corolla was coming towards her on the opposite side of the street. The first thought that entered her mind was that it was one of Jake's bimbos. *Stop it!* She commanded herself. It was always wrong to think so badly of him. Besides, he's too smart to bring them home.

She pulled into the driveway and pushed the automatic garage door opener. As soon as the door had lifted, she pulled her car inside and shut off the engine. She grabbed her things and got out, closing the garage door as she went into the house.

Jake was in the kitchen washing glasses. An alarm bell went off along with the pounding in her head. He never did the dishes. Was he covering up the presence of a woman? Had her original thought been correct?

He turned to face her. "You're home early."

"I'm not feeling well. I'm heading upstairs to lie down."

Vanessa felt Jake's eyes on her back as she left the kitchen. What she couldn't see was the wide malicious smile on his face.

CHAPTER ELEVEN

As Sofia drove away from the Jeffers house, her mind was reeling. She'd never expected things to work out better than she'd even hoped for. Vanessa's husband, Jake, had just offered her the keys to the kingdom, so to speak, and all she'd come for was some financial help. Only, had she heard the man correctly? And could she even trust him? After a moment's reflection, she came to the conclusion that she should. After all, they both wanted the same thing—Vanessa's inheritance.

It seemed so simple. If she joined forces with Jake, she'd never have to waitress again. Nor would dirty old men pinch her ass or try to cop a feel ever again. But, most of all, her feet wouldn't ache anymore. And then there was all that money...

According to Jake's plan, Sofia would take Vanessa's place. She would learn how her sister spoke, capture her mannerisms and simply become her twin. Who would know? Other than Jake, no one knew that Sofia existed.

Jake had prided himself an amateur photographer and over the years had taken countless pictures and videos of Vanessa hosting dinners and fund-raising galas. He hated the fact that his wife was such a goody-two-shoes, always raising money for some charitable cause. "Damn that bleeding heart of hers. Had nobody ever told her that charity began at home?" he'd said, echoing her own thoughts.

And when Jake had finally asked whether or not Sofia was in, her full red lips broke into a wide smile as she extended her hand for him to shake. While she was learning to become Vanessa, Sofia could stay in the condo that Jake rented. *What a win-win situation*, Sofia mused.

***

Jake expected Sofia to become Vanessa overnight. Unfortunately, it wasn't as simple as Jake had imagined. Though it turned out to be a slower process than Jake had wanted, Sofia was a quick study. She watched videos of her twin over and over ad nauseam until she thought her eyeballs would bleed. The only thing that kept her going was the fact she'd soon be wealthier than her wildest dreams.

Sofia found herself both attracted and repelled by Jake. Certainly, he was handsome and well-put together physically, but there was something about him that creeped her out. It was like a sixth sense warning her off. And yet, the lure of the money trumped all her senses. Just the same, she was glad that he'd made no advances towards her. Working with him was far from easy. And she'd nearly walked out at least twice with the desire to return to Rome. The worst time was when they were in the kitchen of the condo. She was exhausted and needed to stop. Jake had pushed her way too far and the scene scared the hell out of her...

"Say it again, Sofia and watch that damn accent of yours."

"Please Jake, I'm tired. Can't we stop for today?"

"Again!" He hissed. "Say the line, *again*."

"I don't want to. Tomorrow's another day," Sofia whined.

Without warning, Jake grabbed her by her shoulders and shook her. "When I tell you to do something, you do it! Do you understand?"

Scared, not expecting such a reaction from Jake, Sofia trembled. However, she was not Vanessa and couldn't be bullied so easily. The fear in her eyes was quickly replaced by white-hot, anger. Jake saw it and realized that he might have pushed her too far. She was the linchpin of his entire plan. The last thing he wanted was to have her walk out on him, so he tried to mollify her.

In a softened voice, Jake apologized. "Forgive me, Sofia. I didn't mean to upset you. It's just that I need this to be over as soon as possible, which means you need to be Vanessa, through and through. There can be no margin for mistakes. Can you forgive me?"

Though Sofia hadn't signed on for all this baggage, she nodded.

"Good. Perhaps you have done enough today. We'll stop here."

After Jake had gone, Sofia poured herself a drink and sat down to think. Jake had just shown her a side of him that frightened her. But, then again, what had she expected. In all honesty, he intended to murder his wife and she would become her. Is this the actions of a nice man? She only prayed that she didn't live to regret it.

***

Several weeks had gone by with Sofia working tirelessly to replace her own mannerisms with those of Vanessa's. Deep down, despite her progress, Sofia feared she'd never truly be ready to pass for her twin. Jake sensed this and cheered her on. He would tell her, "You can do it. No one will scrutinize you. There is no reason to."

"But what if I did something my sister would never do?"

"Like what?"

"I don't know, Jake. If I knew I wouldn't do it."

"Listen to me, Sofia. When I look at you, I see Vanessa. So will everyone else. And if you do blunder, they will think Vanessa's ill or having an off-day. Everyone has them from time-to-time. Why do I know this for a fact? Because no one knows you exist. No one will ever expect she has a twin. Trust me."

To get Sofia to stop double guessing herself, Jake would always finish the pep talk with, "No one is going to come between us and Vanessa's money. No one. This is going to be a piece of cake."

***

As Sofia practiced to become Vanessa, the actual Vanessa was interviewing divorce lawyers. She didn't intend to go up against Jake unless she had the best attorney available. While she was doing this, she continued to act as if nothing was going on. The last thing she wanted to do was alert her husband in any way.

Jake thought that Sofia was ready to replace Vanessa. Only, Sofia didn't agree and balked. She began to pace the living room of her condo, wringing her hands.

"Please, Jake. I need another week, at least. If only to hone my skills. Then I think I'll be ready."

Knowing that he couldn't push Sofia too hard for fear she'd want out, he handled her with kid gloves "I understand what you're saying, but we've got to do it now. The longer we wait, shit can happen. I believe in you. Why don't you believe in yourself?"

"Nerves, I guess."

"Let's make it a trial run. How's about going to Elliot Kastner tomorrow and asking for money? Vanessa did it all the time. If you can fool him, you're solid," Jake suggested as a sort of compromise.

"But...isn't Elliot Vanessa's childhood friend, as well as the administrator of the trust?"

"That's why, if you fool him, you're going to pass as Vanessa," Jake said, using Sofia's own words to help convince her to see Elliot.

Sofia pursed her lips as she thought the matter over. Finally she relented. Only, she had just one remaining question. "What will we do if Elliot senses I'm not his childhood friend?"

"Good question. There's only one answer. "See to it that you *don't* fail."

***

Ever since Sofia showed up Jake had gone into planning mode. He realized that every move he and Sofia made had to be perfect. Anything less would cause his plan to get Vanessa's money to fail. The transition of Sofia into Vanessa had to be smooth and non-detectable. And before Sofia went to speak to Elliot, certain things had to be in place and others dealt with.

First off, there was Vanessa's teaching position at the college. At first Jake considered having Sofia take a leave of absence. But, if Sofia assumed Vanessa's teaching duties, wouldn't it appear to be business as usual? How difficult could it be for Sofia to teach her native language to college kids? Jake smiled at his own innate wisdom. All Sofia had to do was follow Vanessa's syllabus. When Vanessa was asleep, he'd copy it for Sofia to look over. The situation was definitely not a problem.

As for Vanessa's charity work, including luncheons and pretentious galas, luckily, according to her planner, there were none scheduled for most of the month. Sofia would have to be switched a little sooner than planned. Again, no biggie.

It would appear that the most critical problem would be the switch itself. How they would do it had been on Jake's mind since the conception of this plan. He'd drug Vanessa and then bound and gag her until they were ready to take her into the desert seemed to be the best way. She'd remain in the guest room during the short interlude. Then he and Sofia would place Vanessa in an oversized black canvas duffle he had and drive out to the desert. There, he'd shoot her. The coyotes and other wild creatures would pick her bones clean in no time. No one would be the wiser. And Sofia would become Vanessa—for the time being.

Jake thought about how he'd drug his wife. Her father's death made this aspect of the plan easier. The doctor had given her a prescription for Xanax, of which she'd taken only a few. There were plenty of pills left to do the job. Putting them in her green tea after dinner would be child's play.

CHAPTER TWELVE

It was decided. The time to go into action had arrived. After going over the plans one more time, Jake made one change. To him it was minor, but to Sofia it was huge. Instead of going to see Elliot Kastner first to see if Sofia could fool him, Vanessa would be taken out of action. Jake felt it prudent to get Vanessa out of the way so that she wouldn't show up while Sofia was with Elliot.

Of course Sofia was against this change because it destroyed the spirit of compromise that was originally discussed. It also reminded Sofia that Jake was in charge and controlled the destiny of her life. The only good thing was that she didn't have to be around when Jake drugged and bound Vanessa.

Jake called Sofia at 9:45 pm. "It's done," was all he said before hanging up. Sofia knew what she had to do.

***

The next morning, Sofia drove to the house. She expected to see Jake, but he'd already left for work. At least he trusted her enough to be on her own. The first thing she did was to call the college and told them she was ill. That gave her breathing space before she applied for a leave of absence. Next, she called Elliot Kastner's office and told his receptionist that she'd be in to see Elliot around noon. That turned out to be easy.

All morning, Sofia tried on Vanessa's clothes, one item after another, trying to pick something that Vanessa would wear when she went to see Elliot. She was aware that people were creatures of habit and prayed she didn't pick something totally wrong. Finally, after chastising herself for acting like a child, she chose a beige suit.

She styled her hair and put on her makeup as if she were Vanessa. When she was done, Sofia paraded before the full-length mirror looking for any imperfections. Finally, she felt she was ready and grabbed Vanessa's purse and car keys, heading out to the garage. She got into Vanessa's Prius and shook her head with distaste. Why on earth would a wealthy person buy such a ridiculous car when they could afford a Mercedes or Porsche?

Using the GPS, Sofia drove to Elliot Kastner's law office. When she arrived, the receptionist smiled at her and told her to go right in. As she entered, Elliot Kastner rose from his chair to greet her as she walked into his office. Only she didn't hug him hello, but merely sat down in a chair directly in front of his desk. Wondering what was up with Vanessa, Elliot sat back down.

The man sitting directly across from her had auburn hair and beautiful green eyes. He was quite handsome, making it quite easy for her to look at him. His office was quite masculine and yet warm with his book-lined walls and modern paintings of the desert. Sofia tried to take everything in without being so obvious, knowing that Vanessa had been there a thousand times before.

Something was different about Vanessa, but Elliot couldn't put his finger on it. Nor could he explain why the hair on the back of his neck was twitching. He merely smiled at her and asked what brought her there today.

Sofia smiled. "I guess what brings me here all the time— money."

Elliot chuckled. "Do you need extra money this month?"

"Of course," Sofia said, but didn't elaborate. She had to force her eyes to remain on his.

"Things okay at home?" Elliot asked, his eyes never leaving hers.

"Sure, why shouldn't they be okay?" Sofia replied.

"Just asking, no particular reason," Elliot answered.

Sofia bit her lower lip. Elliot thought that was a sign of nervousness. Since when had Vanessa ever been uneasy around him? They'd been friends since God knows when. And what kind of answer about things at home had she given him? They both knew things were bad, otherwise why would she be contemplating divorcing Jake? Something wasn't right here.

"So tell me, Vanessa, how much do you need and when you need it by?"

"$15,000 by yesterday."

"Okay. No problem. How's about some lunch?"

"Not today, I'm afraid. I've got too much to do."

This was totally out of character. Unless either one of them was truly pressed for time, they always went out for lunch. His gut was telling him that something was amiss. He decided to prod her. "I'm curious, what are the funds for?"

"I want to help finance some new equipment for the hospital."

Why would she ask for more money for equipment when she received the money last week for the same reason? "You would have made your mother so proud."

"So it's all set, then," Sofia replied, rising from her chair.

Elliot stood and was about to come around and walk her to the door, but she was already gone. He sat back down and wondered what had gotten into Vanessa.

***

Jake was already there when Sofia let herself into the house. She found him sitting in the kitchen eating a roast beef sandwich. He finished chewing what he had in his mouth and asked, "how did your meeting with Elliot Kastner go?"

"I think it went as well as it could."

"What's that supposed to mean?"

"It means, he agreed to the money. It means that I went in to see a man I didn't know and had to wing it. It means it would have been easier had you had gone with your wife once or twice to see him to know what he was like. That way you could've armed me with more information."

"Hey, calm down. You're acting like you said or did something that triggered that man's radar. Tell me it isn't so."

"Nothing like that. He merely sat there staring at me as if I was some kind of specimen on a slide."

"That was probably your nerves reacting."

"No. I'm telling you the man looked at me with laser eyes. I felt as if everything I did or said was coming under scrutiny."

"Vanessa once told me that Elliot Kastner was the most cautious man when it came to her money," Jake offered.

"But he wouldn't be overcautious with Vanessa, unless he was paranoid."

"The only way to prove is it all went well, Sofia, and that is to check Vanessa's account. Let's see if the funds were added."

Sofia followed Jake into Vanessa's tidy home office and over to her desk. He sat down and booted up her computer. After waiting several moments, the login for her trust account appeared. Jake keyed in a sequence of numbers and letters. The screen changed and he was in. He highlighted and opened the latest entry, a deposit of $15,000, which Sofia had requested.

Sofia's face brightened. "He did believe I was Vanessa."

"Yes, he did. He would have never authorized the money if he hadn't. And if he could be fooled, the rest of the world could be fooled as well."

"Does that mean we can get rid of Vanessa?"

"We're taking care of that tonight."

***

Elliot Kastner was almost certain that the woman who'd come to his office that day was not Vanessa. She said things that Vanessa wouldn't have and acted as if she hadn't known him for a lifetime. His imagination ran wild with possibilities. It was almost as if some alien being possessed Vanessa's body. Either that, or she had some long-lost twin out there that finally showed up. Seriously though, it could've been her doppelgänger. Though he couldn't recall where he'd read it, supposedly everyone had a person who resembled them somewhere in the world. If not that, call him paranoid, but he believed that the person who sat before him in his office was a stranger who might have gone under the knife to have her face remodeled to look like Vanessa. The reason, of course, had to be to get control of her trust fund. His blood froze. Was it possible that Jake was behind this?

His entire body tensed. The bottom line was this: if it wasn't Vanessa who came to see him, where was the real Vanessa? That question totally unnerved and frightened him. Okay. Reality check. Was any of this even possible? Maybe.

Crazy as it seemed, Elliot wouldn't – no couldn't rest until he knew the truth. He had to know what the hell was going on. He reached for his phone.

CHAPTER THIRTEEN

Vanessa opened her eyes. It was dark. Flat on her back, she couldn't move either her arms or legs. They were bound. Nor could she scream for help. Her mouth was taped shut. Panic rose from the pit of her stomach. Beads of sweat popped out along her forehead and drenched her armpits. She felt herself dissolving into fear as the blood flowing through her veins turned to ice. Before she lost all control, she valiantly struggled to rein in her galloping emotions and try to help herself..

She tried to concentrate on her surroundings. Rocking her body, she discovered she was lying on a mattress in a room. Could it be a room in her own home? She thought back to the last thing she could remember. Having tea. She'd been with Jake. Had it been last night? Or had she been here in this place longer? Had Jake put something in the tea? Had he done this to me? *Good Lord, why?* Her heartbeat sped up again and she felt the panic returning. The unspoken answers to her questions were frightening.

Sounds outside the room became more audible. She could hear a muffled conversation elsewhere, but couldn't decipher what was being said. The voices grew louder and were coming towards her. The door opened...

***

Frustrated with not having made any headway with Jake Jeffers, Olivia Simmons had put her quest on hold. Her obsession with Jake had threatened to overcome her. Finally, she was driven to see her psychologist who counselled her to find a distraction. She decided to find a substitute and embarked on a forty-two day cruise around the world. On the cruise she hoped to snare a wealthy, old man with her charms. When that bombed, as well, she fixated once more on Jake.

However, Jake was too preoccupied with getting Sofia ready to step into Vanessa's shoes to notice. He had no inkling that Olivia Simmons was stalking him.

Fortified with several fingers of straight vodka, Olivia Simmons headed to the Jeffer's home in Fountain Hills. She parked in the shadows a half block away. There were no street lights lit to ruin the night sky, so she took a small tactical flashlight with her to see where she was stepping. The area was known for rattlesnakes, and the like. Nor did she want to trip and, heaven forbid, break a leg or hip.

Olivia made it to the Jeffers house without any mishap and walked around the house looking for lights. She saw light on the side of the house on the first floor and stealthily moved towards it as she kept safely out of sight behind bushes. Her binoculars suspended by a chord around her neck banged against her chest each time she took a step. She raised the binoculars to her eyes and saw Jake talking and gesturing to his wife. She replied back and then Olivia saw Jake nod that handsome head of his and then they both left the room.

***

Jake and Sofia were discussing what to do next with Vanessa, who was lying unconscious and bound in one of the guest rooms. He'd wanted to take her out to the desert before she gained consciousness. Sofia wanted to talk to Vanessa at least once. She wanted Vanessa to know that she had a twin sister. It would be a rude awakening for Vanessa to learn that life as she'd known would still go on without her.

"Let's get this over with, the sooner the better," Jake said again.

"No one knows this is happening, so why the rush? We have all night. Besides, maybe she's already awake. When was the last time you checked on her?"

Jake shrugged. "I haven't looked in on her in a while."

"I want to go with you."

Jake agreed. Actually, he wanted to see the expression on Vanessa's face when she saw Sofia, as well. It definitely would be quite the Instagram moment.

Vanessa trembled as she saw the door slowly open, the light illuminating Jake and...a woman who looked exactly like herself! Her throat closed as a flood tide of questions crowded her mind, but before she could even take another thought, Jake turned on the light and they entered the room.

Vanessa tried to resist, but lacked the strength to prevent Jake from scooping her up and slinging her over his shoulder. He carried her out of the room into the living room and propped her up on the sofa. She trembled with fear as it freshly washed over her and permeated every pore. *She was probably going to be killed and could do nothing to prevent it. Why else is that woman here, if not to replace me? How did he get her to look so perfect?*

Vanessa's eyes widened as the woman began to speak. "Hi, Vanessa. My name is Sofia and I came all the way from Rome to be here with you—well, that is, for the last few minutes of your life."

Vanessa glared at Jake, who turned away. *Coward*, she thought. *In the end he was proving himself to be a wuss.*

The woman snapped her fingers. "Over here, Vanessa, I'm talking not him. You're probably wondering who I am. I'm not a mere lookalike. Nor did I have plastic surgery. I am your twin. We were separated at birth and adopted by different people. Only, my parents were poor, not rich like yours. That's why I'm here today. I will rectify that mistake. I promise to make you proud," she said and began to laugh.

Vanessa tried to process what the woman had said. Had her father known that there were two babies? If he had, why hadn't he told Vanessa? How she wished she'd known about her twin's existence. She had little time left in her life, the life she'd wanted to spend with Elliot. Elliot will discover that the other woman wasn't her. If anyone could tell the difference, it would be Elliot.

"Let's get this thing done," he said. "There's only so many hours left before dawn and we don't know how long it will take."

"I'll get the bag," Sofia offered and left the room.

Outside, Olivia's hands were shaking as she watched the activity in the room. Were her eyes playing tricks on her, or were there two Vanessa Jeffers?

Why was one trussed up like a Thanksgiving Day turkey? She burped. It reminded her about how much vodka she'd had imbibed before coming here tonight. But, whether or not she was drunk mattered little. Even with her alcohol-addled brain she could see that bound woman was in a heap of trouble. She had to call the police. Where had she put her phone? Then she remembered that it was in her purse in the car. Olivia turned to go back to retrieve it and stumbled on a rock. She fell down the slight incline and hit her head on another rock, rendering herself unconscious.

Sofia returned toting a large, black duffle bag. Vanessa's heart leapt into her mouth when she saw it. She didn't have to be a genius to deduce that she was going to be stuffed inside. *Did Jake hate her that much? Probably not. He just loved her money more.*

Claustrophobia kicked in as Jake began to zip close the bag. It went hand-in-hand with the panic that had already co-opted her body and mind. She tried to scream, but couldn't. Her mouth and throat were as dry as the desert. She sensed that they were heading there.

All Vanessa had left was prayer. Mentally, she began to recite the Lord's Prayer.

CHAPTER FOURTEEN

Jake and Sofia drove several miles from his home into the Sonoran Desert. He turned on his brights to see where he was heading. The last thing he needed was to get a flat. He chose to enter an area that wasn't open to the public. After driving several miles, Jake stopped the car in a desolate area overgrown with cacti and a variety of other desert plants and bushes. Vanessa had been placed into a large duffel bag, which was now stowed in the trunk of Jake's Lexus. His intention was to shoot her and leave her there. He doubted anyone would come across her body until the land was converted into homes or shopping malls decades from now.

"Is this Indian land?" Sofia asked Jake.

"Doubt it. The Indians own a great deal of property, but I don't think they own anything around here. Why do you ask?"

"I just thought it would be a bad time to get caught trespassing, that's all."

"This isn't the Wild West. They don't scalp people anymore. They just arrest you. But, we should hurry, just the same. The sooner we get home, the better I'll feel." Jake opened his car door and Sofia opened hers. They met at the trunk of the car.

Jake reached inside and grabbed one end of the duffel. "You take the other end and help me lift the bag out."

"I didn't think she was this heavy," Sofia complained.

"That's because she's squirming. I knew we should have kept her drugged for a reason. Just lift your end. We'll lose the dark soon."

As they walked into the thicket of cactus, a coyote howled in the distance. Sofia dropped her end of the bag.

"I intended to shoot her, not bash her brains in."

"Very funny. I'd like to get this over with. It's scary out here."

"Afraid of the dark, Sofia?"

"No, only the creatures lurking in it. Can't we just do it here?"

"I guess this is as good a place as any," Jake said. "I doubt that anyone could see her from the road and it's the middle of nowhere."

Sofia gladly let her end go. She was more scared of what was out there than going to hell for murdering her own sister. Then again, when she decided to come to Arizona she didn't think she was going to help murder her twin. It might have been nice to get to know Vanessa. Now, she'll never have the chance.

Jake interrupted her thoughts. "Here hold the flashlight steady for me so I can see what I'm doing," he said, handing the high-intensity beam to her. He removed a pistol from his jacket and aimed the gun at the duffel bag.

Sofia couldn't help but notice his shaking hands. Obviously, Jake didn't go around killing people all the time. The coyote bayed again and spooked Sofia. She jumped.

Jake snapped at her. "Hold the flashlight steady!"

"I'm trying."

"Well, try harder."

Finally, Jake pulled the trigger in rapid succession three times. The bag danced momentarily on the ground with each bullet that hit it. The noise had been deafening and its echo could most likely be heard a great distance away. The bushes rustled near them.

"Let's get the hell out of here," Jake said.

They both got back into the car and Jake started the engine. Driving back to the house in Fountain Hills, neither said a thing for several minutes. Finally, Sofia broke the silence. "What now?"

"What kind of question is that?" Jake said sharply.

"A logical one, I think."

"No one asked you to think," Jake snapped.

Sofia roared back. "I just helped you kill and dispose of your wife. Do you really want to treat me so poorly?"

Jake got the implied message. "Sorry. I'm just on edge. I didn't think it would affect me so badly."

"I understand, but keep in mind, I'm now your partner in more ways than one."

Again, Jake picked up on the subtle hint. He needed to keep her happy for the time being. "Since you're now Vanessa, you'll have to live with me in the house. Every so often, you'll hit Elliot Kastner up for money, which we will split, until you're thirty-five and Kastner is no longer the administrator of the trust. How's that for a plan of action?"

This mollified Sofia, for which Jake was glad. Truthfully, he hadn't expected to be so affected by Vanessa's death. Obviously, he had to get a better grip on his emotions. He needed to find a way to rid himself of Sofia before she became an albatross dangling from his neck. Originally, he thought he would keep her around for the five years until she turned thirty-five, but now he doubted he'd be able to. If he could convince the world that Vanessa was dead from some kind of trauma, then the money would be his sooner and he could purchase that villa in Mexico that he had his heart set on.

"Jake, wouldn't it be prudent for me to cut back on some of my charitable work? I could cite health reasons."

He caught the tail end of what Sofia had said. "What?"

"I figured since I'm now Vanessa that it would be safer if I didn't put myself out in the public as much. Less exposure would lessen my chances of making mistakes."

Jake mulled over what Sofia had said and found he had to agree with her logic. Less presence equaled less chance of being discovered as a fraud. He began to see the usefulness of following such a path, especially if he used the excuse that Vanessa was ill. Then her sickness could very well lead to her untimely demise. Dear Sofia might have just conjured up her own death. Bless her little heart.

"You're right. Perhaps the next time you see Elliot Kastner, you can look ill. Fool him and you fool the world."

Sofia imagined she'd be taking Vanessa's place as Jake's wife. That would mean moving into the house and completely immersing herself in her twin's identity. It would be a difficult task, but the rewards were great. For Sofia, it was a dream come true. She'd have all the fancy clothes and toys she always desired. Snatching fervent glances at Jake, who appeared to be concentrating on the road, being his wife didn't seem so bad. After all, the man was quite attractive. Perhaps in time, he'd desire her. Amusedly, she thought, the things *people did for money and comfort.*

Jake hated the sight of Sofia. It was a constant reminder of Vanessa. The sooner he'd rid himself of Sofia, the better. He needed to come up with a foolproof plan to murder her and make it look like an accident or suicide. Then, all the money in the trust fund would be his.

84

CHAPTER FIFTEEN

Orin Plummer III lived in the Sonoran Desert not too far from Fountain Hills. Born into a banking family, he was bred to take over the reins of the family business when the time came for his father to retire. From boarding school to Harvard Business, he was groomed only to be a banker. After graduating from Harvard, it took all of six months as the head of a small bank in Fountain Hills for him to realize this was not what he wanted to do with the rest of his life. So he joined the Army against his father's wishes despite the fact he had been threatened with disinheritance.

More than anything, Orin had longed to be a biomedical engineer. He wanted to be the guy who designed systems and products for the medical field like artificial organs or devices to replace human body parts. He'd taken physics, chemistry, and biology during his four years in college, but still needed other necessary courses, like organic chemistry and physiology. He felt that he could enrich his education by enlisting into the Army. While there, he trained as a medic and found that he enjoyed the work and remained in the army for three tours.

When he returned to the family home in Fountain Hills, his father expected him to go back into banking. He felt it was time for him to retire and pass on the control of the family business like his own father had. Only Orin had different plans. He wanted to get a job as a nurse and do medical engineering on the side during his free time. This angered his father who disinherited him. Only his old man couldn't touch the trust Orin's grandfather had set up when Orin was born.

Orin moved out of the family mansion and found a small condo near the Southeast Veterans Affairs Health Care Clinic in Gilbert where he was able to work while he trained as a nurse. There he met a woman he thought loved him as much as he loved her. Unfortunately, it turned out that she loved what he'd inherit being a Plummer more. When she discovered he only possessed a small trust fund, she moved on to a more affluent surgeon.

This devastated Orin. He proceeded to drop out of society which took more than a year of preparation. First, he had to find the perfect place to shut himself away from the world. This he found deep in the Sonoran Desert not too far from the family mansion. The area was virgin territory and completely isolated. With a design for a house that used passive solar principles instead of conventional heating and cooling systems, he cleared three-quarters of an acre and built his dream house. He harnessed the sun for electricity and used several different methods of maintaining an adequate water supply, including drilling a small well and capturing water from the air at night and rain during monsoon season. For food, he had a small vegetable garden and hunted the wildlife that lived in the area.

Orin had reinvented a life for himself in the desert based on his own rules and desires. Isolated from the trials and tribulations of the outside world, he was quite content to be on his own. Until the world encroached upon his little slice of the world.

Outside, deep in the desert, Orin was hunting game for the next day's dinner, when he heard the unmistakable report of gunshots fired in rapid succession. Having another hunter in his part of the desert unnerved him, so he headed in the direction the shots came from to find out what was going on. He hadn't gone too far when he heard the slamming of car doors, indicating that he'd come close to the only access road in and out of the desert.

Continuing on in the same direction, Orin now detected the acrid smell that lingered after a gun had been fired. He knew he was close. Somewhere in the distance, a coyote howled, answered by another. Then it was quiet again, except for the crunching of his boots. He went just a little further and the pungent smell of nitroglycerin stung his nose. This is where the gun had been employed.

Orin slowly scanned the area around him with his mag light until the strong beam fell upon a large, black duffle bag. He bent down to examine the bag more closely and saw that it had been riddled with three bullets. A dark liquid, which he assumed to be blood seeped through each one. Something had been stuffed inside and shot.

Still crouching, Orin slowly unzipped the bag. As Vanessa's face came into view, he exclaimed, "Jeezus!" Who would want to kill such a beautiful, black woman and leave her body to be picked clean by the coyotes?

He removed a glove and placed two fingers against the woman's carotid artery. His heart turned over when he felt a pulse. She was still alive, but he might not be able to save her. Her wounds could be too severe and she might bleed out before he got her back to his house. He studied her wounds. The most serious wounds were in her chest and thigh. He took off his belt and using it as a tourniquet, cut the flow of blood from the wound in her thigh. He stuck his bandana in the chest wound and rezipped the bag up to her neck to protect her from twigs and rocks.

There was nothing more he could do for her out there and every minute he delayed was a moment of her life ebbing away. Determined to do all he could for the poor woman, he put his glove back on and grabbed hold of the straps securely. Then he pulled the bag behind him through the path he'd come, as quickly as possible, praying the bag didn't fray apart from the friction.

Orin reached the house and got the bag inside and placed it on the floor next to the rectangular, kitchen table. He rushed to the closet where he kept his linens and grabbed several towels and sheets. Then he got the supplies he'd need from a well-stocked supply of medical products he'd had in case he got hurt. Luckily for the woman he was prepared.

The sheet was placed on the table. Then he bent to unzip the bag. Judging from her expensive-looking clothing, the woman wasn't homeless. Gently, he cut away the bag where it stuck to the woman. When she was completely free of the bag, he slid it from under her body and carefully lifted the woman onto the sheet. He cut away the rest of her clothing so he could examine her wounds more closely.

She had a bullet wound that creased the side of her head. "Lucky girl," he muttered. The other two were more serious. A bullet had entered her body above her left breast and was still lodged there. The third bullet went straight through her right thigh. It missed her femoral artery by less than an inch. Whoever shot this woman obviously couldn't face her and shot through the bag. And didn't check to see if she was dead.

Orin went into action. He removed the bullet in her chest. It hadn't hit any vital organs, but the woman was going to hurt for some time until the wound healed. He stitched and bandaged it. Then he cleaned, stitched and bandaged her thigh. Again he thought about how lucky she was that her would-be murderer missed the femoral artery.

The last wound he had to tend to was the deep gash on the side of her head. The bullet grazed her scalp pulling chunks of skin and hair from over her left ear. Orin shaved the hair from around the bullet's path and cleansed it. Then he stitched the gash closed. He mopped the sweat beads from his forehead and then took her vitals. Her pulse was better, but not great. He'd done all he could, so he passed the baton onto a higher power. Hopefully, she'd regain consciousness soon.

After brewing a pot of coffee, Orin sat down in a chair near the table to watch the woman. He was used to long hours of little or no sleep. In the army, he sometimes went 36 hours straight. He feared that if he wasn't vigilant and she went into distress, he wouldn't be able to save her. Therefore, sleep was out of the question until she was out of the woods.

***

Olivia Simmons regained consciousness. Dizzy and disoriented, she had no idea where she was or why she was lying amongst the rocks and shrubs in the dark. She had double vision and found it difficult to walk, so she crawled as best she could out of the hollow she'd fallen into, practically shredding her Chanel silk dress. She remembered where she was and what she'd seen earlier. Only, now she was no longer certain about what she'd witnessed. There was one thing she was sure of and that was getting away from there before Jake Jeffers returned and discovered her.

***

Jake was taking off his jacket when he remembered the gun. He had to get rid of it. He reached into his pocket for it, but it wasn't there. *Probably fell out in the car*, he thought, as he headed for the garage. Sofia watched him go out. When he returned several minutes later, his face was as pale as if he'd seen a ghost.

"What's wrong?" Sofia asked.

"Did you see the gun?"

"No. You had it. Why?"

"I can't find it. It's gone."

"What do you mean, gone?" Sofia asked, looking apprehensive.

"What part of that, did you not understand?" Jake snapped.

Sofia ignored his caustic remark. "Could you have dropped it by the bag?"

"There's no other explanation, I'm afraid."

"Don't go to pieces. It was in the middle of nowhere. No one is going to find it."

"You better hope they don't."

No, Jake. You'd better hope they don't. The gun has your fingerprints on it, not mine.

***

Late morning the following day, the black woman stirred. When she began to softly moan, Orin, who'd just gotten up to stretch his legs, hurried back to the table. He saw her eyelids flutter for a few moments, then open and close in rapid succession in order to clear her vision.

When Vanessa was eventually able to focus, she saw a slender man of medium height with a scruffy brown beard and a bushy ponytail. His complexion was ruddy and lined, but his light blue eyes were as sharp and crystal clear as a lake. Her eyes widened as she tried to scream and get off the table.

"Whoa, stay put, ma'am!" Orin said grabbing her shoulders. "You'll rip out your stitches!" Then in a more soothing voice as he eased back her shoulders, "Please lie back down. No one's going to hurt you. You're safe here."

Vanessa acquiesced, but didn't appear to be any calmer. Orin knew he had to gain her trust or she was going to bolt again at the first chance she got. "Would you like some water?"

She nodded.

"Okay, but you have to remain calm so you don't fall off and hurt yourself. Will you promise to do that?"

Vanessa nodded again and Orin got her a glass of water, which he held for her to sip. As she drank, he told her his name and where he found her. "Do you remember how you got there or who shot you?"

She gestured to the glass of water. He gave her a little more before setting the glass down.

"I told you my name. I'd like to know yours?"

"Vanessa Jeffers." Her voice sounded raspy, but Orin understood her. "Are you a doctor? What am I doing here?"

"I live here in the Sonoran Desert. I was out hunting wild game last night and heard gunshots. Remember, I told you that. I once was a medic and trauma nurse. Now what about you. Can you tell me how you got shot? What happened to you, Vanessa?"

She blinked her eyes rapidly and wet her lips with her tongue. Orin could plainly see the pain in her eyes, but aside from her physical pain, he detected another kind, more emotionally raw in nature.

"Who shot you, Vanessa? Orin asked softly. "Who left you to die in the desert?"

Tears slipped from Vanessa's eyes. Orin gently dabbed them away with a tissue.

"My husband," she whispered. She repeated it louder. "It was my husband."

CHAPTER SIXTEEN

Orin was appalled. "Your husband shot you and left you for dead?"

"Yes."

"Good God, woman! You're lucky he was such a coward and shot you through the bag."

Only Vanessa had begun to drift off. He was hopeful that she would pull through, but then what? By saving her, he put himself in a most tenuous position. He couldn't let her leave. She most likely would tell people about him and where she'd been. There was absolutely no way he'd trust her not to blab. That would be the end of his seclusion. He'd worked so hard to create this little sanctuary and now it was on the brink of destruction.

He could ask her to remain with him, but something told him she was more of a city-kind-of-girl. He couldn't force her to stay. Why would he save her only to make her life a living hell? Thus, Orin had no idea how this damned if you do—damned if you don't situation he'd put himself in would play out. The only thing he was certain about was that he wouldn't freely allow his isolated space to be invaded and have to rejoin society.

As he watched Vanessa sleep, erotic thoughts entered his mind. He hadn't experienced such feelings in a very long time. He hadn't wanted to be with a woman since his doomed affair. In fact, such thoughts never crossed his mind—until now. He didn't need the useless distraction of those feelings that the sleeping woman was stirring within him.

Gently, he brushed the errant strands of hair that had fallen on her beautiful face. How could any man want to hurt such a lovely woman? The terrible things people did to one another was one the reasons that drove him from society.

Orin went to his refrigerator and took out a pot of rabbit stew. Using a ladle, he scooped out just enough to fill a bowl and warmed it on the stove. When it was warm to his liking, he brought it over to the chair facing Vanessa and began to eat. It would be so easy to fall in love with such a woman he thought and then laughed at possessing such a crazy notion.

***

The following morning, before Jake headed out to his office, he needed to speak to Sofia. He found her in the kitchen sipping coffee and reading the newspaper. "You've got a full day ahead of you."

Sofia looked up at the well-dressed man standing before her. He *was* devilishly handsome. She could understand women turning their heads when he passed. "What do you mean?"

"Now that Vanessa's gone, you're going to have to slip into her shoes, both figuratively as well as literally. You can't be going back and forth from the condo to the house. Fill up the car with all of your personal items and bring them here. I will take care of closing the condo."

"All right, I'll do that this morning."

"Make certain you fulfill all of Vanessa's appointments and learn everything there is to know about her pet projects."

Sofia sighed.

"You knew you'd have to do this when you agreed to help me murder Vanessa," Jake reminded her.

"I know, but—"

"No buts. Just get everything done. You can start by looking through her planner and calendar. Right now, we're the only ones who know that Vanessa is dead. I'd like to keep it that way."

"I understand," Sofia acceded.

"Good. Make certain you do," Jake said and walked out of the kitchen. A moment or so later, she heard the garage door open and close.

Sofia wasn't at all thrilled with Jake's attitude. She was his partner, not his servant. In fact, he acted as if he intended to cut her out of the deal and that made her damn nervous. Who could she complain to? The police? That would go down swell. *You see, officer, my partner reneged on our deal to kill his wife and share her trust fund.*

She finished her coffee and put the cup in the dishwasher. Then Sofia headed for Vanessa's office. It looked like it had been designed by Martha Stewart. The shutters, carpeting, and furniture were color-coordinated in red and white, and everything in the room was organized and neat.

Sofia sat down at the white desk with its matching white-cushioned chair and pushed the white laptop to one side. She opened the top drawer and found Vanessa's planner. She opened it to the present date and discovered that her sister had very little listed. She had a dentist appointment the following week and Sofia thought it best to cancel. A dentist would be able to spot all the differences with their teeth. She wondered if she should do the same with the hairdresser and nail salon. Cancelling everything for now would probably be best. Putting the book aside, she went through the other drawers, locating her checkbook, monogrammed notepaper, all sorts of paper clips, pencils and an eraser. There were extra multicolored Post-its to replenish the ones in the white ceramic cat Post-it holder, which Sofia found adorable. A twinge of regret washed over Sofia. She and Vanessa probably had a great deal in common and could have been good friends... Now she'll never have that.

Fortunately, the regret that Sofia felt was fleeting and she pushed the negative thoughts aside. Rising from the chair, she walked into Vanessa's massive closet. She looked through the overwhelming amount of dresses and shoes that filled the oversized carpeted room. Her paltry amount of dresses wouldn't fill up one wall. How had Vanessa managed to choose one dress out of all the lovely things to wear each day? It was like picking an outfit from a clothing store. Momentary anger clouded her mind. *All this should have been mine, not Vanessa's. I should have been adopted by the ambassador.* However, the anger quickly dissipated when she remembered every single one of those dresses were now hers.

***

From the very night that he shot Vanessa in the desert, Jake had been thinking of a way to rid himself of Sofia. He found her annoying and a constant reminder of Vanessa. Her presence simply unnerved him. Jake normally felt no guilt over any of his actions. If he had, he couldn't possibly have done certain things that helped make him the ruthlessly effective lawyer that he was. But this was different somehow and the only way for him to successfully purge himself of this feeling was to permanently remove Sofia from his life. Besides, he didn't want to share any of Vanessa's money with her. He'd waited six long years to finally get his hands on it.

Jake thought he'd devised a solid plan that would work. There was no room for failure. Not only would he be free of Sofia, but he would also be free of Vanessa with the world as his witness, thus paving the direct path to the trust fund legally.

CHAPTER SEVENTEEN

Elliot waited for Vanessa to come the following week for lunch. He had to know whether or not the Vanessa who walked into his office was his Vanessa. When he hadn't heard from her, he suspected that something wasn't right. His original fears about Vanessa being ill resurfaced and he gave her a call. Sofia, who now possessed Vanessa's cell phone, answered. The caller ID indicated that it was Elliot Kastner. She had to be careful not to slip up.

After taking a deep breathe, Sofia answered. "Hi, Elliot."

"How are you, Van? I expected to see you this week. What's going on?"

"Sorry. I've been really busy. In fact, I'm on my way to a luncheon."

"Don't you have class in a bit?"

"Sure, sure I do, but I decided to take a short leave because I've been so busy," Sofia recovered. "When do you want to have lunch next week?"

"When will you be free?"

"Wednesday. Let me double check my calendar. Yes. Wednesday is good. What time?"

"Let's shoot for noon."

"Where do you want to meet?"

"Come to my office. We'll take one car." Elliot said. "See you on Wednesday."

"See you then," Sofia replied and the connection was broken.

Elliot hung up the phone convinced that he hadn't been talking to Vanessa, but someone doing their best to impersonate her. There were too many inconsistencies. Vanessa never would ask what time to come. They always met at noon. She knew the place, his office. These were things that a stranger wouldn't know. He'd already dragged his feet way too long. He had to do something. But, he had absolutely no idea what or how to go about it. For advice, he'd go to his childhood buddy, Hank Davis, who was a detective on the Phoenix police force.

They met at a sports bar in downtown Phoenix. Elliot got there first and ordered a beer. Sipping his beer as he waited for Hank to arrive, Elliot glanced up at the TV above the bar. It was tuned to the local news. He nearly gagged on the beer.

A reporter was standing at the spot where Vanessa Jeffers's car skidded off the road and plunged sixty feet down an embankment. When the medics arrived, they pronounced her dead. The reporter droned on...

Tears filled Elliot's eyes. His Vanessa was gone... dead. How was this even possible? Then a crazy thought passed through his mind. Was the dead woman really Vanessa or the person who was impersonating her? Holding his head, he waited for Hank.

***

Jake watched the news report from his office. He'd been so careful in his planning of the *accident*. There was no way, even if they did an autopsy, the authorities will never know that the woman in the car had been dead before the impact. Thanks to the movies and TV, it was such child's play. There was no reason for an autopsy if the authorities accept the crash to be an accident. Being Vanessa's identical twin, Sofia shared the same DNA, including fingerprints. To all who knew Vanessa, the corpse was hers. Finally, the inheritance was his.

CHAPTER EIGHTEEN

As Orin nursed Vanessa back to health, she saw the innate goodness in the man and wondered what traumatic event occurred that drove him to hide from society and live in such a desolate place. He was too kind and too talented a healer to be hidden away. She knew at least a half-dozen hospitals that could use a man like him. An optimal moment to ask hadn't come up until a week after he saved her.

Vanessa's wounds still hurt, but were healing. She'd begun to walk short distances to the bathroom and back to the bed on her own. When Orin needed to go out hunting and left her on her own, she borrowed a book from his small library. From the eclectic selection of books, she could tell he was a complicated man, far from being shallow. His intelligence and apparent knowledge of the world was evident when he spoke to her. She became more and more curious about him as the days passed.

One night as they shared a rabbit stew that Orin had put together from the rabbits he'd shot the night before. Vanessa looked at the man that sat before her. With a shave and a haircut he'd be quite attractive. Though he was strong and exuded strength, he could be just as gentle. Again she wondered what his story was.

"Orin, I hardly know a thing about you."

"There's nothing more to know other than what you see. I am a simple man who wants nothing from anyone."

"An educated man like you doesn't hide from the world unless he feels he has no choice. What drove you to such a strident decision?"

Orin studied her a moment. "Why do you care?"

"Because... because I think you're too good a person to hide yourself away here."

"Who said I was hiding?" Orin said, looking directly into her eyes.

"Me."

"Vanessa, you don't get it. I like it here. I came here because I wanted to live off the land like my forefathers."

"Do you *really* like it here? Or have you merely convinced yourself that you do?"

Orin rolled his lips and said nothing. Mindlessly, he pushed his stew around the plate with his fork. Vanessa thought that she may have overstepped and struck a nerve. She suddenly regretted having prodded him. Obviously, the man didn't want to discuss his life with her. Therefore, it would be cruel for her to push him to do so. Especially after he saved her life. She was about to change the subject when he spoke.

"I've built a fairly comfortable home here carved out of the wilderness. Did you know that you're the first person I've spoken to for nearly five years?"

Vanessa shook her head, but said nothing, sensing it was more of a rhetorical question than anything else.

"When you asked what caused me to run and hide, you forced me to think about things I haven't thought about for years."

"Please don't continue if you find it painful," Vanessa said, reaching for his hand.

"I think I'm able to talk about it now. At least I can be more rational now than I was then."

Vanessa nodded. "Okay, but if you change your mind, I'm all right with it."

Orin told Vanessa about the woman he'd loved and how she'd turned all his dreams into one huge nightmare. She could relate and told him so.

"If I could go back in time, Orin, I definitely would have chosen Elliot. We spent one night in bliss together, but I knew I loved him. However, Jake entered my life at school and I fell for the con man, trashing the love Elliot and I shared. One night I had too much to drink and before long I discovered I was pregnant. I couldn't disgrace my dad and married him. Not too far down the road I realized that Jake never loved me—only my money. So our situations aren't so different, but our reactions to them are. You chose to run and cut yourself off from the world. Well, the world is still out there, and so is the lucky lady waiting to meet you who'll love you for who you are and not what you might possess. Don't squander what you could give to others, Orin. When I'm all healed, please come back with me."

Orin shook his head and got up from the table. He began to pace. "I can't. I just can't."

"Okay. I understand. I won't pester you about it again," Vanessa said contritely.

"But neither can you."

Vanessa's head snapped up and her eyes met his. The expression on her face was a mixture of shock and confusion. "What are you saying?"

"I simply can't allow you to leave here—"

"I give you my solemn word that I will tell no one about you or where you live."

Orin shook his head. "How will you explain how you survived three gunshot wounds on your own? And how will you prevent Jake from attempting to do the job right this time?"

"I'll think of something. I have no choice. I cannot live out here. I'll lose my mind."

"What you don't seem to grasp is the fact that you have no choice," Orin said.

"Are you going to lock me up and keep me a prisoner?"

"No. I don't need to. You'll never survive on your own out there. I can almost guarantee you'll never make it to the main highway."

"If I am determined enough, I will."

"Do you think I saved your life so you can get killed out there?" Orin asked.

Vanessa said nothing. He continued. "Why can't you remain here with me? Am I so repulsive?"

"Good heavens no! You're a wonderful guy, someone I owe my life to, but I'm a city girl. I've never had to rough it and got accustomed to the finer things in life. And honestly, I don't want Jake to get his hands on my money. Can you understand that?"

"Again, if you go back you will put yourself in the cross hairs of danger."

"I realize that, Orin. Elliot will protect me. I know he will. Please consider what I'm telling you. Let me go back. *Please!*"

CHAPTER NINETEEN

Vanessa Jeffers' funeral, coming on the heels of her own father, made society news. Jake Jeffers, the grieving husband, was emotionally distraught and on display for the entire world to pity. That is, everyone except Elliot, who was certain Jake was hiding something. Whether it was the fact that the woman being buried that day wasn't Vanessa, but a doppleganger, or God knew what. With Jake, anything was possible. However, there was one thing Elliot was certain about. Jake would come to his office and request a transfer of ownership of Vanessa's trust fund.

As Elliot sat in the back of the church listening to the priest conduct the mass, his mind drifted back to the happy times he and Vanessa spent together. He pictured her red pillowed lips and longed to be able to kiss them. How he longed to enfold her in his arms and hold her as he nuzzled her swanlike neck. Tears slipped from his eyes with the reality of that never happening again. Surely, Jake and that imposter killed his beloved Vanessa. He swore to prove that Jake Jeffers was a murderer, even if it was the last thing he'd ever do. He'd get justice for Vanessa.

***

Several days later, Jake went to see Elliot. During the entire drive over to Elliot's office, he thought about Vanessa's trust fund and how it could have been more sizable had she not handled it so poorly. Her donating the money to charity was a waste, primarily because charity began at home. He felt that you only went around the world once. Why not strive to have a better trip? Had Vanessa not given so much of her money away, things might have turned out differently between them. Then again, probably not. The woman was such a goody-goody and far from practical, which was a flaw in her genetic makeup. But most of all, he found her boring in bed. Why else would he continually look elsewhere?

Now with the infusion of Vanessa's money, he could make a new start for himself on the beaches of Mexico or the Bahamas. That had been his dream all along. Now it was becoming a reality.

Jake walked into Elliots's office without an appointment. He marched up to the receptionist's desk. She was already past her prime, being a non-descript forty-something. He would never have such a person being the first face a prospective client saw upon entering the law office. She should have been replaced by a younger, more attractive woman. Better window-dressing stimulates the growth of business. He identified himself and was told to have a seat.

After keeping the man waiting for nearly thirty minutes, Elliot buzzed his receptionist and had her usher Jake into his office. It took nearly every ounce of control he possessed not to grab the man by his throat and throttle him. Elliot wanted to rearrange Jake's face permanently. But he remained civil.

Elliot rose to greet him, forcing himself to shake the man's hand. To take the step beyond that and offer his condolences nearly proved impossible, but he managed to mumble the words which caught in his throat. Instead, he wanted to ask the monster standing before him what he did to Vanessa. He gestured to the chair in front of his desk. "Have a seat and tell me what brings you here today."

Jake raised an eyebrow, an indication that he knew Elliot was well aware of his reason for coming. "Now that Vanessa is gone, I'd like to have her trust transferred into my name, being her sole survivor."

Sounds fitting for the person who murdered her and now wants to pick at her bones. "Okay, but no-can do."

Jake's face darkened. "What! It should be a snap. Are you trying to pull something here?"

"I was afraid you'd react this way and told Vanessa so—"

"What the fuck are you talking about? I'm her beneficiary."

"Not anymore. Vanessa changed that about a month ago. Her new beneficiary is the Children's Hospital."

"You've got to be shitting me," Jake said, his face reddened with anger. "That bitch is giving all her money to a hospital?"

Elliot got up and went over to a filing cabinet nestled in a corner. If he hadn't, he would have punched Jake for speaking about Vanessa like that. Seething, Elliot opened a drawer, began to thumb through several binders until he found the one he was searching for and pulled it out. He carried it back to his desk and placed it before Jake, the proper page already bookmarked. "Here is what you need to see."

Jake pulled the binder closer, his expression remained clouded in anger. After glancing at the stipulated page, the anger transformed into hostility. "You told her to do this, didn't you?"

"I assure you that I had nothing to do with her decision to do this," Elliot said, struggling to keep his expression passive.

"Really? Then please explain to me why Vanessa removed me, her lawful husband, as her sole beneficiary."

"As you well know, Vanessa and I were close childhood friends—"

"Cut out the oratory and give me a straight answer."

Elliot tented his fingers and leaned forward. "You want the truth, well here it is. Vanessa came to me several months ago. She was very upset and told me that she was going to divorce you—"

"That's a crock of shit!"

"No, Jake. That's the cold truth. She suspected you of being unfaithful and simply wanted out of the marriage. I asked her if she was certain and she told me that she'd been considering it for some time. Those are the facts. You can choose to believe them or not. That's your prerogative. However, I'm legally bound to transfer the trust funds to the hospital."

"Did Vanessa cut me out of her will, as well?" Jake asked in a quieter voice, though his eyes remained hard.

"All I can say until the will is formally read is that she had me draw up a new one," Elliot said, enjoying inflicting a little pain in the other man's day.

Jake shot up out of his chair, slamming his palms on Elliot's desk, startling him. "Goddamn that woman! How could she do this to me?"

"I know that's more of a rhetorical question, but I do have an answer. I guess it was easy after you had a vasectomy and let her believe she was infertile, and found it difficult to keep your Johnson in your pants. For some women that's enough."

Jake's eyes narrowed to slivers. "You piece of shit! You're really enjoying this, aren't you?"

"When you hurt someone I love, yeah. What goes around comes around," Elliot said as he walked toward the door. "I have real clients to see. Now if you'll get the hell out of my office, I can get some work done."

Jake moved so quickly that he stubbed his toe. He hadn't taken more than five feet before he turned to face Elliot. "This isn't over. I intend to fight the transfer."

"Fine with me. Just remember, though, until I receive a restraining order, Vanessa's trust will be transferred to the hospital."

Without another word, Jake turned back and stormed out the door. He hadn't even asked when the formal reading of the will would be, Elliot mused, as he sat wishing he had throttled the man after all. Knowing he'd murdered the love of his life, Elliot felt he was a coward to let Jake continue to breathe fresh air above ground.

Eleanor Jones, Elliot's receptionist watched Jake Jeffers storm out the door and broke into an unabashed grin. *Good for you, Elliot,* she thought, pushing back her chair and heading toward his office. She hadn't liked the smug, arrogant man and the way he looked down at her and spoke to her as if she were trash.

She knocked and poked her head into Elliot's office. He was sitting with his hands clenched, staring at nothing in particular. "Are you all right, Elliot?"

He looked at her. "Yes...yes, of course."

"Good. That man is bad news."

"You got that right."

***

As Jake stomped out to his car, he vowed to get the bitch's trust fund one way or another. It was a matter of principle now.

CHAPTER TWENTY

Orin watched Vanessa heal and gain back her strength with trepidation. Remembering her unfavorable feelings toward remaining there with him, he knew that one day soon she'd revisit that same conversation concerning her desire to leave. It was inevitable. He was faced with a no-win situation, but also knew that he had to let her go. She'd already gone through hell and back. To force her to remain, which was not actually possible without physically restraining her, was inhumane. Despite the fact he'd grown to love her, he was preparing himself to accept losing her. And nearly a month-and-a-half from the night he found her, she was serving the stew Orin had made and started the dreaded conversation.

"Orin, I'm feeling good thanks to your care. I think I'm strong enough to go back."

"Where will you go? Back to the man who did his damnedest to murder you?"

"No, of course not. To Elliot. He'll protect me," Vanessa replied. "Besides, I love him and I know he feels the same about me."

"Can he protect you 24/7?"

"He'll find a way—I just know he will."

"And what about your husband? Will he let you live in peace with Elliot?"

"He'll have to. I could always go to the authorities and have him arrested for attempted murder. The fact that I can do this at any time should keep him at bay. Besides, he's probably conniving a way to steal my inheritance away from the children in the hospital who need it so badly. I must stop him from doing such a terrible thing. That money must help the sick children. Don't you see that?"

"Yes, I can and do understand, but is it really worth your life? You've been given a second chance. Why tempt fate again by going back?"

"Because I must. If I remain here I'll go nuts and take you with me. This lifestyle is not for me. I need the city and all its trappings. Can't you see that? I'm honestly not cut out to be here. Please reconsider letting me go. And while you're at it, think about returning with me and working at one of the hospitals I'm affiliated with. They'd be lucky to have you."

Orin had stopped eating and was staring down at his plate. Vanessa wished she could see the expression on his face. She needed a clue to what he might be thinking. She wasn't certain if she should continue or desist. Beating the subject to death could not be such a good idea. The suspense was killing her so she broke the silence. "Orin?"

Orin looked up. His eyes were misty. He definitely wasn't happy about what she'd said. However, Vanessa had one last thing to say. "Orin, I owe you my life. But, more than that, I care about you a great deal. I just can't remain here indefinitely. Surely, you already know that."

"I do, Vanessa. When I made the decision to save your life, I planted the seeds of this conversation. I have grown to care a great deal about you, as well. That is the main reason why I want you to remain. Underlying this reason is another. Though you promise never to reveal my existence here, you may slip and do so, just the same. However, the bottom line is that only a selfish and cruel man would imprison you here. I am neither."

Vanessa's face flushed with heat as she felt a warm glow flow through her. *He's going to let me go!*

"I have a motorcycle hidden to be used for emergencies. I will take you to Elliot's place only on one condition. That he is home to let you into his home. I will not leave you to wait for him."

"All right. He's home most evenings, so perhaps you can take me then?"

Orin nodded. "Oh, there's one more stipulation."

"Yes?" Vanessa said.

"You must never come back looking for me."

"I understand, Orin. When I leave, it's goodbye."

***

It was decided that Vanessa would leave later that night. Not many people were up and about at two-thirty in the morning, but even so, Orin feared someone might recognize her. To prevent this from happening, she wore a helmet with a visor. As soon as the helmet was secure, she got on the bike behind Orin and wrapped her hands around his middle. Once more, he explained his game plan. "I'm going to stop a short distance from your friend's place. If he answers the door, I'll take off. If not, I'll bring you back to my house. Got that?"

"Yes," Vanessa said. *Please be home, my love.*

"Good." Orin hit the gas and they were off. He felt Vanessa snug against his back and enjoyed her closeness.

Butterflies fluttered in Vanessa's stomach. She hated giving Elliot such a shock, knowing he thought her dead. And what if he was away on vacation?

Once they got to the main road, it wasn't that long a ride to Elliot's condo in Scottsdale. When they reached the beginning of his block Orin pulled to the side of the road and Vanessa got off the bike. She threw her arms around Orin and kissed his cheek. "No matter what, I will always be grateful to you. There's no way I could ever forget you." She kept her head close to his for several more minutes as tears filled her eyes.

It was Orin who pushed her away. "You'd better go."

Reluctantly, Vanessa gave him one last hug and began to walk.

He watched as she walked the rest of the way and rang the doorbell of a two-story stucco and stone villa with a double wrought-iron door. A light came on and the front door opened. Orin turned to leave. He couldn't bear to stay a moment longer.

CHAPTER TWENTY-ONE

"I'm coming! I'm coming! Hold your horses! This better be important. You've got some nerve waking me up at this hour!" Elliot called out as he rushed down the steps, nearly missing one.

The doorbell chimed again just as Elliot yanked the door open, yawning. Instantly he was wide-awake. His beautiful, long, thick lashes Vanessa always envied flew up as his jaw dropped. A beat or two passed as he stood there wide-eyed and tongue-tied, staring at Vanessa. Disbelief filled his eyes before the reality of the moment permeated his brain.

"Oh. God! You're alive!"

Elliot pulled Vanessa inside, closing the door behind her. He immediately enfolded her in his arms. Tears of joy filled his eyes and streamed down his cheeks. Vanessa pressed her face against his bare chest and breathed in the scent that was his alone. They remained like that for several minutes, slowly rocking together as he murmured into her hair, "Thank you, God, thank you, God."

When they ended their embrace they sat down on the sofa in his great room. Elliot couldn't take his eyes off of her, afraid that if he did, she'd disappear. "How is it possible that you're not dead?" Elliot asked. "Surely, Jake would have done away with you when he had the chance. All he cared about was your money."

"It's quite a story. But, before I explain, I want to thank God for blessing me with a second chance at life to correct my biggest mistake. Leaving you."

He took her hand and kissed it. "I still can't believe you're sitting here with me. I thought I lost you forever."

"First off, Elliot, tell me what happened to my twin sister, Sofia."

It was then he realized that the woman in the casket had been this Sofia. "She's dead. No more than a week ago, Jake held a funeral mass for you. Supposedly, you were killed in a fatal auto accident. Now I know it was your twin and not you in the casket."

"They had worked out a deal between them, which of course, Jake reneged on. He probably promised to split my trust fund with her in exchange for her helping him kill me. First, I was drugged and then put into a large duffle. Then Jake drove to the desert and shot me three times through a zippered bag. He never opened the bag to see if I was dead. Lucky for me, he didn't hit any vital organs. I was found before I bled out by a man who nursed me back to health. He brought me here tonight."

"That fucking bastard. I'd love to choke the living daylight out of him with my bare hands. As for the superhero that saved you, I'd love to shake his hand," Elliot said.

"I'm afraid that can never happen. I swore an oath to my good Samaritan never to reveal his identity or where he lives. I owe him my life and I will never break this promise."

"Did you know you had a twin sister?" Elliot asked.

"No. I truly regret not knowing her."

"Despite the fact she helped Jake try to kill you?"

"Yes. It's unfortunate that Sofia met Jake first and not me. Things might have turned out differently."

Elliot chortled. "With Jake around I doubt the outcome would have been any different. How do you think she found out about your existence?"

"I gave this a great deal of thought. It was most likely when my father died. The funeral was televised, especially in Rome, where I think she said she was from."

"I suspect Jake had been planning your death for some time."

"Why do you say that, Elliot?"

"Because, if your twin came from Italy, she'd have an accent. When she came to my office to request money, she spoke without any trace of an accent. She obviously didn't learn that over night. However, she didn't fool me because she was too formal and acted as if we hadn't known one another all our lives. Even if she was a better actress, she still would have lacked your warmth."

"It's so obvious now that when Jake told my twin she was needed to fill my shoes, he meant to publicly air my death. That way all of the money would go to him."

"Only, he had no idea until yesterday that you had changed your beneficiary to the children's hospital," Elliot said, grinning.

"Yeah. That certainly sucks for him. He went to all that trouble for nothing."

"He's already threatened to fight it."

"Sounds about right. I would love to see him pay for what he's done," Vanessa said.

"So would I, but how are we going to prove any of this? Your twin's death was declared an accident, despite the fact she was impersonating you."

"Elliot, how much do you want to bet that somehow Jake was behind that accident? He probably fiddled with the car."

"There's another possibility, Van. He could have drugged Sofia just like he did with you and ran the car off the road down the steep incline. That way, if they analyzed the car they'd find no evidence of tampering."

"Whatever the case, my sister's death was no accident," Vanessa said, pushing every word through clenched teeth. "We can't just do nothing. Jake needs to be punished for the horrible things he's done."

"I agree, but we need to speak to someone with the knowledge of how to proceed from here. Do you remember Hank Davis?"

Vanessa tried to put a face to the name, but for the moment couldn't. She shook her head. "How can he help us?"

"Hank's a detective with the Phoenix police. If anyone knows where we go from here, it's him."

"Oh, I certainly hope so, Elliot. To think that Jake nearly killed me, but succeeded with Sofia and will probably walk away from both horrendous deeds scott-free makes me sick."

Elliot drew her near and kissed the top of her head. "We'll find a way to make him pay. For what he's done to you, alone, makes me want to kill him myself. No matter what, I love you and always will. And nothing or no one will ever hurt you again. This I promise." He cupped her chin and tilted her face toward his and lowered his mouth to hers.

When their lips met, it was like the first time so long ago when they were kids in college high on life and love. The kiss grew in intensity and duration. When it ended, Elliot held her face in his hands and began to kiss every possible place on her face before slipping his lips down to her slender neck.

Vanessa had slipped her hands around his neck, twisting her fingers through his thick auburn hair. Their kisses became feverish and intense again quickly and Elliot slipped his hand under the sweatshirt Orin had given Vanessa to wear. A soft moan rose from her lips. But, as he began to lift the sweatshirt, Vanessa grew rigid and cried out, "No! Don't!"

Elliot was confused for the moment.

With tears filling her eyes, Vanessa explained. "I don't want you to see the ugly, puckered scars, the bullets left."

"It's all right, baby. I always will love you no matter how you look. Please trust and believe in me."

Vanessa relaxed her body, but kept her eyes tightly closed. Elliot surmised that she didn't want to see his first reaction, just the same. Gently, he pulled the sweatshirt up and over her head. The skin was red and puckered over her left breast. He bent to place butterfly kisses all over her chest.

Vanessa let out a sigh, but tiny tears had slipped from her eyes. Elliot kissed them away before continuing down her body. He pulled off her jeans and saw the ugly-looking scar on her thigh. He hated Jake more for scarring her beautiful body. Again, he swore a solemn oath to himself. If it was the last thing he'd ever do, he'd make sure Jake was severely punished.

Vanessa reached out and pushed Elliot's pajama bottom passed his thighs. She stroked his rigid cock and helped guide it inside her. For Elliot, the planets were finally in alignment. She was his now and forever. Knowing she felt the same way made it all much sweeter. Together they moved to a place only they knew.

The tempo of their movement increased and Vanessa turned her head from side to side, moaning. At this rate, he was going to come. He couldn't wait for her. With a deep groan he grew rigid and ejaculated. Not two minutes later, Vanessa raked his back with her fingernails as her body began to spasm. A long moan confirmed she'd had an orgasm. They clung together a few more minutes before they went upstairs to his comfortable bed.

Once again, they made love. This time it began slow and sweet. Tender kisses and slow hands. Certainly, that's how it started, but they were now celebrating life and attempting to make up for all lost time. Their kisses became more like the smoldering heat that joins metals. Soon they were trying to devour each other's lips. Then each fought for domination to be on top. When they finally became one, the intensity of their coupling had grown exponentially and the orgasms the experiences simultaneously were explosive.

***

Elliot's alarm went off, but not wanting to disturb Vanessa, who was snoring softly next to him, he quickly killed its shrill tone. Slipping out of bed, he went downstairs to call his receptionist to let her know he'd be in later. There were several things he had to take care of first. He went to the bathroom and then got back into bed.

***

Hank Davis rang the doorbell of Elliot's condo at 12:15. Elliot shook his hand and led him inside. "Thanks for coming, Hank. We certainly appreciate your advice on this precarious situation we find ourselves in."

"Where's Vanessa?" Hank asked, looking around for her.

Gesturing with his chin towards the stairs, Elliot said, "Upstairs getting dressed. Let's go into the kitchen. I have coffee brewing."

Vanessa came down the steps wearing a beat-up pair of shorts that nearly reached her knees and a tee. Hank noticed her first. "No matter what you wear, you're still that hot chick I had a crush on in junior high."

She flushed. "Thank you, Hank." Turning towards Elliot she added, "How could I ever forget a sweet guy like him?"

Elliot poured each of them a cup of coffee and sat down. "Okay, Van, tell Hank the entire sordid story."

Vanessa told the detective everything. He didn't interrupt once. When she was done fifteen minutes later, he asked questions and then gave them his advice.

"That is quite a story. Though Jake is guilty of several crimes, the D.A. could have a problem prosecuting him."

"What?" Vanessa blurted out. "How is that *even* possible?"

"There's no smoking gun, excuse my pun. There's no hard evidence connecting Jake to shooting you. You have no witnesses to collaborate your story."

"It's not a *story*. It's fact. I have the scars where he shot me," Vanessa said.

"Anyone could have shot you."

"But what about Sofia, her sister's death?" Elliot interjected.

"Remember, that was ruled an accident. Though, then again, her existence might help sell your story to a jury and the D.A. could get a conviction on circumstantial evidence. But, I'm curious, how do you think he'll react when he finds out you're alive, Vanessa?"

She shrugged. "He'd be furious and probably apprehensive about me going to the police."

"Exactly. Would he be enraged enough to try to silence you permanently?" Hank asked.

"I don't know. Jake's a sociopath, but with him, anything is possible, though there's the chance he'll run to save his hide."

"My guess is that if he think's there is an easy way to get at Vanessa without getting caught he might attempt to kill her," Elliot said.

"From how you've described him, I agree with Elliot. If we pick him up now, he'll know Vanessa's alive. There's absolutely no other reason for us to arrest him. My concern is that he'll make bail and become a loose cannon. That would be dangerous for Vanessa. Therefore, we've got to find a way to get Jake to incriminate himself."

"So what do you propose, Hank?" Elliot asked.

Hank thought for a moment. "Doubt is a very powerful weapon. Let's use it against Jake. Get him to doubt himself. Tell him she's alive, but in a coma. Maybe he'll go to the hospital and make an attempt on her life. Then we'll definitely have him. The downside is that he'll realize the jig is up and run to some place where we can't touch him. How we go from here is up to you, Vanessa. What do you want to do?"

CHAPTER TWENTY-TWO

As Jake's receptionist transferred Elliot's call, he thought it strange to hear from him. "Mr. Kastner, what can I do for you? Are you ready to transfer the trust into my name?"

"Not quite, Jake. Since technically you're still Vanessa's husband, you need to know that she was found alive in the desert. It looks like someone shot her and left her for dead. She's in a coma at Banner University Medical Center in Phoenix and when she wakes up—"

"You're shitting me. Is this some kind of a sick joke?"

"No joke, Jake. Vanessa is alive."

"How could she be? You saw me bury her."

"Chalk it up to a miracle. After all, doesn't God work in mysterious ways?" Elliot said and hung up.

Jake wore a path in the carpeting of his office as he mentally digested what Elliot had said. *Was it possible for Vanessa to have survived? After all, he hadn't really checked to see if she was dead. No, she's dead. And, there's no way that someone found her and saved her. She was shot in the middle of nowhere...Then, why else would Kastner call? Does he suspect me of having killed both women? Is this just a play to get me to incriminate myself? No one even knew about Sofia's existence. Except Kastner. Did he suspect that the woman who came to his office wasn't Vanessa?... But, what if Kastner is telling the truth? What if somehow Vanessa is alive? How could he have prepared for something like that? There was no way he could have foreseen this happening,* he thought, running his hands through his hair. *Well, it had, and now he had to damn well deal with it.*

What alternative did he have? There was no way he could turn himself in to the authorities and hope for the mercy of the court. He'd already murdered one woman, whose funeral was televised around the world, and attempted to murder another. There would be no mercy. He had to assume the worst. That left him with only one viable solution. He had to take whatever money was available and disappear to a place that had no extradition laws with the United States.

To the best of his knowledge, there were several places he could take refuge in, but only two were viable, Cuba and Canada. Cuba, because it was a country that refused to cooperate with the United States whenever possible. Joanne Chesimard was a prime example. She'd been an activist and a member of the Black Liberation Party who was convicted of murder in 1977. She escaped from prison and fled to Cuba. As for Canada, they won't send anyone back to the US if the death penalty is on the table.

Jake rationalized that if he didn't leave a paper trail he might be able to find a place to hide in Canada until it became safe to move to a more permanent place. He always thought that it was a good idea to stash some extra money and clothes for a rainy day and had kept close to $750, 000 in his office safe along with a phony passport and license. Well, they might be coming for him soon, so the time was now. He had to get out of Dodge, ASAP.

The cash he secreted in a money belt he wore around his waist under his shirt, while the clothes he needed were packed in a small duffle bag, He drove his car to the airport and left it in the long-term lot. Then he donned sunglasses and a baseball cap and took a taxi cab to the closest Amtrak station in Phoenix. Over the next week he slowly made his way to Vancouver, using both Amtrak and thruway connecting services. There he purchased a used car and drove leisurely to Saskatchewan. He doubted anyone would look for him there, so he rented a small house in Saskatoon. Exhausted, he finally relaxed and rested up. He had a great deal of time to kill.

***

Even though the police had set a trap for Jake in case he came around to silence Vanessa, she knew deep in her heart that Jake had run as far away as he could, He was nobody's fool. Neither were the authorities. They waited two days for him to show up at the hospital. When he didn't they issued an All Points Bulletin to nab him.

Jake eluded capture, avoiding a nationwide APB, though his Jaguar had been found in the long-term parking lot at the Sky Harbor Airport in Phoenix. The authorities concluded he could be anywhere at this point and finding him now looked doubtful.

"Jake's probably laughing his head off on some tropical island in the Pacific," Vanessa said to Elliot as they were having dinner at a quiet little restaurant, not far from his condo. With Jake most likely thousands of miles away, she was able to leave the safety of Elliot's place.

"The world has become a smaller place due to modern technology. There's virtually no hiding. He'll slip up one day and the authorities will nab him, Van. You'll see," Elliot replied, reaching into the bread basket for another piece of bread.

"Not if there's no extradition, but one must never lose hope, I suppose."

"At least, he'll be out of your life and divorcing him will now be easy."

"I guess that's my silver lining," Vanessa said, before sipping her iced tea.

"You sound down. What's wrong?"

"The very fact that Jake killed my twin before I got to know her greatly bothers me."

"Don't forget that she played a starring role in trying to kill you."

"True, but I don't really think she signed up for that. Jake can be very persuasive," Vanessa reminded Elliot.

"Yes, that's true. However, Jake's not here now, but I am and I'm offering decadent chocolate cake with your coffee," Elliot teased.

"Where were you with the cake when Jake proposed to me?"

They both laughed at her inane statement. At least Elliot was able to take the edge off of Vanessa's previous disturbing thoughts.

"Actually, Elliot, I don't want any dessert. Instead, I'd like to go home and celebrate life."

A crooked little smile appeared on his face. "Yes. That's a wonderful idea."

CHAPTER TWENTY-THREE

Jake began to relax his guard somewhat living in Saskatoon, considered the largest city in the Canadian province of Saskatchewan. It was damn cold, but at least the people were pleasant. The best part was that no one knew him here. He felt safe. All he had to do was to remain here for a year or two until it was okay for him to travel to Mexico. Then he could live the life he always wanted to. When he closed his eyes, he pictured the gentle sway of the palm trees in the warm wind and the hot sand as he watched the gorgeous women strolling past him, all for the taking.

He'd sometimes go into town to pick up the newspaper, buy groceries, and grab a quick meal. For exercise he took long walks. One day he found he couldn't sleep and got out of bed much earlier than usual. He dressed and headed into town for a leisurely breakfast.

***

Alan Stanfield was sitting and enjoying his breakfast of pancakes, scrambled eggs, sausage and toast as he completed the daily crossword. This was one of the few pleasures he could now afford since his divorce. Thanks to the bloodsucking lawyer his wife hired, he got fleeced. There was no way he'd give the bitch the small nest egg he'd secreted away when she was already taking the house and most of their bank accounts. The divorce itself was quite spectacular and newsworthy. It destroyed his standing in the community, making him a pariah. Accused of molesting his daughter, he could no longer hold his head up high. To avoid giving her one more cent and to save face, he fled to a place he could hardly pronounce. It wasn't too bad living there once you got used to the friggin' cold.

The bell on the front door of the small eatery clanged as a tall man clad in an overcoat wearing a ball cap and sunglasses entered. Almost immediately the hair on the back of Alan's neck prickled. There was something about the man that triggered such a response, but Alan had no clue as to why. He watched the man amble over to a small table and sit down. The waitress acknowledged him and placed a menu on the table. The man removed his sunglasses to look at the menu, but before Alan could get a good look at the man the waitress returned with a mug of coffee and blocked his view. She remained there writing down his order. Finally, she moved away and Alan got a good look at the man's face. He nearly gagged on the piece of toast he was swallowing.

He knew that face. How could he forget the face that belonged to the lawyer who destroyed his life? It was that bloodsucker, Jake Jeffers. The bastard in the flesh. What was he doing here? No one ever came to Saskatoon for pleasure. He, himself, was a prime example. His gut told him that Jeffers had to be running from something and came here to hide. Jeffers was the reason Alan had to flee the land of his birth and start a new life in Canada. And now he intended to teach Jeffers that payback could be a bitch. He intended to find out what Jeffers had done and then call the authorities back in Scottsdale, Arizona to let them know where they could find Jeffers. For the first time in ages, Alan Stanfield felt good—really good.

***

Elliot and Vanessa were honeymooning on the beautiful Hawaiian island of Kauai. They were renting a private villa and enjoying the solitude. Sheltered from prying eyes, they made love and swam in the pool. Lying on chaise lounges, sipping Margaritas in the midday sun was their norm. Then they'd make love until dinner time and stroll along the beautiful beach.

"This is heaven as far as I'm concerned, Van. Me and you together on this beautiful island."

"I should have divorced Jake right after I discovered he'd deceived me. Thinking about all that lost time saddens me."

"Don't be sad. We'll make up for all the time," Elliot said as he reached for her hand and kissed it.

From the look on Elliot's face, Vanessa knew he wanted to make love to her. Only it was at that moment that Elliot's cell phone chirped.

"Do you have to get that?" Vanessa asked, thinking they might be able to save the mood and make love after all.

Elliot looked at the caller ID. "It's Hank. I think I should take his call. I'll put him on speaker. Hey, buddy, you're on speaker. What's going on?"

"We got him! We got Jake! Vanessa you're going to get the justice you seek."

She jumped out of her lounge chair. "That's great news, but where was he hiding?" Vanessa asked breathlessly.

"A place in Canada called Saskatoon. We were able to convince the Canadians to send him back."

Elliot took her hand in his and squeezed it gently. "How were you able to find the bastard?"

"Believe it or not, we received an anonymous phone call telling us exactly where to find him."

"He probably pissed off somebody's spouse," Elliot said.

"He'd made it an art form," Vanessa added.

"Yeah. That man certainly knows how to make lasting friends," Hank said, sarcastically. "Well, enjoy the rest of your honeymoon. See you when you get back."

"I think we should celebrate and go out tonight," Elliot said.

"But first, I'd like to pick up where we left off," Vanessa said, reaching for Elliot.

The End

Epilogue: Two Years Later

Vanessa awoke early. Propped on one elbow, she watched Elliot sleep. Lying there, he looked younger than his thirty-six years. She noticed a smile on his face and wondered if he was dreaming. That in turn brought a smile to her face as she hoped the dream was about her. In the last two years, the time they'd been together, Elliot had made her so happy. It was easy living with him and she doubly regretted having married Jake prior.

Now, as she watched him sleep, she thought about all the novel ways she might break the news that she was pregnant. She'd nearly given up the hope of having a child. After she had her miscarriage she couldn't conceive for the longest time until by accident she discovered that her ex-husband had had a vasectomy. Now her dream had come true and she was going to share the wonderful news with the love of her life, her soulmate, who'd never given up on her. Such moments, even as mundane as this, filled her heart with joy and she wished she could remain here like this forever. But, as she well knew, forever was a very long time.

Elliot stirred and opened his eyes. Smiling, he reached for Vanessa. She gladly slipped into his arms. He kissed her lips gently, but the kiss deepened and Elliot moved on top of Vanessa. She guided him inside her. Waking up to sheer pleasure was easy to get used to, she thought as they found their rhythm. Vanessa savored Elliot's touch and kisses as he moved inside her. Every stroke brought her closer to bliss.

Their movements quickened and soon Vanessa felt as if she might implode and dissolve into molecules of sheer pleasure as her orgasm began to build. And then suddenly, it was upon her, engulfing her in pleasure. She cried out and her cry was answered by a guttural moan. Elliot had come, as well.

The brilliant Arizona sun had chased the night away and was now dominant in a lazy, deep-blue, Saturday morning sky. Snuggling together, limbs still entwined, their vitals soon returned to normal. Vanessa knew it was the right time to tell Elliot about the baby. No theatrics, she'd just come right out and tell him. She stroked his cheek, smiling. "Elliot, there's something you need to know."

Alarmed at once, he rose on an elbow to see her better. "What's wrong?"

Her smile turned into a huge grin. "Why should something be wrong?"

He relaxed, his features softened. "You're right. I know we've been happy these last two years."

"I think you're going to be happier—"

"Tell me all ready!"

"I'm pregnant."

"What? Did I hear you correctly?"

"Yes, sir, you did."

As the last word passed Vanessa's lips, Elliot was hugging and kissing her as if he'd not seen her for years. After that display of emotion, he stopped abruptly to ask, "Are you certain?"

Vanessa burst out with laughter. "Yes, hon. One-hundred percent positive."

"When are you due?"

"The beginning of November. Happy?"

"You're kidding, right?" Elliot asked, taking her into his arms once more. "I'm over the moon."

His reaction had mirrored her own. With Jake hating kids, she never thought she'd ever be a mother. Now, having this baby will complete her life with Elliot. She was ecstatic.

Speaking of Jake, it had made the front page of their local newspaper. Giving credence to the old saying, what goes around comes around, Jake got his just desserts. Turns out, he was stabbed by an inmate in the prison shower. The man who'd wielded the shiv had been one of the husbands who was on the losing side of his divorce decree. Jake had helped his wife shaft him and he'd merely wanted to return the favor.